Disney

CINDERELLA

CINDERELLA

ADAPTED BY
ELIZABETH RUDNICK

PaRragon

Bath • New York • Cologne • Melbourne • Delhi
Hong Kong • Shenzhen • Singapore • Amsterdam

This edition published by Parragon Books Ltd in 2015

Parragon Books Ltd
Chartist House
15–17 Trim Street
Bath BA1 1HA, UK
www.parragon.com

ISBN 978-1-4723-8838-4

Printed in UK

Dearest Reader,

If you would be so kind as to indulge me, I would like to tell you a tale. Years have passed since these events unfolded, but I remember them vividly. It's no surprise, really. After all, I am a fairy godmother, and fairy godmothers have great memories (not to mention impeccable fashion sense). Over the years, I have helped many young people discover that dreams can come true. I've watched love blossom and grow, watched heroes find strength and hard-hearted people find soul. But this story touched me more than all the others.

It begins, as all the good stories do, with 'Once upon a time....'

Prologue

*O*nce upon a time, there lived a handsome man and a beautiful woman. They were kind, gentle and generous to all. The man worked hard to make his wife happy, and his wife loved him wildly. They lived in a quaint home in the middle of a beautiful kingdom.

A large meadow behind the house provided flowers through spring and summer, and in a small field, sweet lambs grazed beside contented cows. It was a home filled with cheer. When the husband and wife had a perfect baby girl, the home became happier still.

They named the baby Ella, and from the moment she was born, she was their princess.

True, she had no title or crown or castle. But she was the ruler of her own little kingdom. The forest and meadow were her borders, and the birds in the air and the animals in the fields were her subjects.

Whether she pretended to be an elephant traipsing through the Sahara or a wild horse galloping through the meadow, everyone, from the mice in the house to the cooks in the kitchen, was happy to play along. Both animal and human alike fell under her enchantment, happier when in her presence.

Chapter One

*S*pring had arrived in the kingdom. The grass in the meadow was a bright green, and flowers grew tall in their beds. Baby lambs grazed in the meadow, while little ducks flapped around in a small fountain near the main house.

Stepping through the front door, ten-year-old Ella inhaled deeply and smiled. She reached into her pocket and closed her small hand round the breadcrumbs she had brought from the kitchen. She skipped towards the ducks splashing about and began throwing the crumbs into the water.

The ducks pecked at the bread, thrilled to have a treat. But they were not the only ones who wanted some. In an instant, sparrows flew down from the nearby trees, and even the goats and sheep began to make their way over. Soon it was chaos as all the animals and birds tried to get to the bread.

Ella waded among the throng, moving some of the bigger birds out of the way. "You there," she said to one particularly large duck, "what do you think you're doing? Let the little ones have their share." Turning towards a goat with a rather large clump of grass in his mouth, Ella added, "Goliath, do take some time to chew your food. We don't want you getting an upset stomach."

A gentle laugh surprised Ella, and she turned round. Her mother was standing nearby, an amused expression on her face. "Do you still believe that they understand you?" she asked.

A look of doubt filled Ella's bright blue eyes. "Don't they?"

"Oh, yes," she assured her daughter. "I believe that animals listen, and speak to us, if only we have the ear for it. That is how we learn to look after them."

A big smile spread across Ella's face. Then she frowned. "Who looks after us?"

"Fairy godmothers, of course," her mother answered.

(Forgive the interruption, but I can't resist. I was always fond of Ella's mother. Such a good judge of character, and clearly cleverer than most humans. But do go back to the story....)

Ella's eyes grew wide. "And do you believe in them?"

"I believe in everything," Ella's mother replied.

Ella was quiet for a moment, her mother's words running through her head. She nodded. "Then I believe in everything, too."

"Which is just as it should be," her mother declared.

Just then, Ella heard the sound of hoofbeats coming up the drive. She knew those hoofbeats. Ella let out a squeal before taking off across the meadow, heading for the drive. Her father was home!

Ella's father was often gone for long stretches of time on merchant business, and when he was away, the house was just a little less bright.

"Papa!" Ella shouted, skipping the few remaining steps that separated her from her father. "Welcome home!"

Ella's father lifted her into his arms, nearly squishing her in a giant bear hug. She hugged back as hard as her little ten-year-old arms would allow. Then she took a deep breath, inhaling the smell of road and dust that accompanied her father whenever he returned. She loved the smell, even though she knew Mother would force him into a hot bath as soon as possible.

After several moments, Ella slid to the ground. As was part of her routine, she stepped up to Galahad and affectionately put her hand on his muzzle. The horse leaned into her. When Ella turned back round, her eyes widened with excitement. Her father was holding out a beautifully wrapped gift.

"What is it?" Ella asked eagerly.

"Oh, nothing but a cocoon," her father replied. "I found it hanging on a tree."

Ella raised an eyebrow. She knew it wasn't *just* a cocoon. Her father was teasing her.

Ella's father gently shook the gift. "But I *think* there may be something inside." He held out the package, and very carefully, Ella unwrapped the gift. Then she let out a delighted gasp. Inside was the most beautiful and marvellous toy butterfly she had ever seen. With a practised move, Ella's father took it and made the creature flutter around Ella's face. It looked like it was alive!

"In French," her father explained, "that is *un papillon*."

Ella repeated the phrase, the words funny on her tongue. Her father had been teaching her French whenever he was home, and she was slowly becoming more fluent. He said that a true lady knew the language of the poets as well as the language of the farmer.

"*Très bon,*" her father cried after she had repeated the phrase several times. Then he held out his hand. "*Voulez-vous danser, mademoiselle?*"

"*S'il vous plaît!*" Ella exclaimed, dipping into a curtsy. Her father smoothly swept her into his arms, and they began to waltz their way up the rest of the drive to where Ella's mother waited, a happy smile on her face.

Later that night, Ella lay tucked in her bed. The butterfly sat on the bedside table in a place of honour, while her mother sat on the covers, holding a beautiful book. Her gentle voice filled the room as she told Ella a story about a faraway land, a large ogre and a dashing prince.

Ella's eyelids fluttered as she tried to stay awake. Looking down at her sweet daughter snuggled in her arms, Ella's mother began to sing a familiar lullaby. "Lavender's blue, dilly dilly. Lavender's green.... When I am king, dilly dilly, you shall be queen...." Her voice drifted off as Ella's father entered the room. He placed a gentle kiss on his daughter's forehead. Smiling, Ella's mother began the final refrain. Ella woke and her soft voice joined in: "Lavender's green, dilly dilly. Lavender's blue.... You must love me, for I love you."

As the song came to a close, Ella's parents stood up and began to blow out the candles one by one. Walking to the doorway, they turned to take another look at their sleeping angel. In that moment, everything seemed as it should be. They knew themselves to be the most fortunate people, to live as they did, and to love each other so.

However, sorrow can come to any kingdom, no matter how happy. And so it came to Ella's, for her mother grew very ill.

Hovering in the doorway of her father's study, Ella looked on as the doctor examined his patient. A bed had been set up and her mother lay on it, a shell of the beautiful woman she had once been. With his examination complete, the doctor began putting away his tools.

Ella nervously picked at her dress. Her eyes fell on the curtains, drawn against the bright sunshine outside, and she felt a pang of anger. It didn't seem right for the sun to be shining when things were so horribly wrong.

"Ella. Come."

Hearing her father's tired voice, Ella hesitated before walking into the makeshift sickroom. The doctor put a hand on her shoulder as he departed. She knew he was trying to be reassuring, but it just made the sick feeling in her stomach grow stronger. Ella made her way to her mother's bedside and kneeled down, carefully placing her hand on top of her mother's.

"Ella," her mother said, her voice weak. "It seems it is time for me to leave. And we must say goodbye before I go." Tears began to run down Ella's cheeks. "I don't want you to be sad," her mother said. Then she paused and a small smile spread across her face. "Well, you can be sad for a little while. But then, whenever you think of me, I want you to smile. Because I'll be smiling, too, when I look at you."

Ella's throat closed up and she struggled to say something. But words wouldn't come. So instead she just nodded.

Her mother nodded back. "I want to tell you a secret – a great secret that will see you through all the trials that life can offer." Ella leaned in, as her mother's voice was now barely a whisper. "You must always remember this:

have courage and be kind. You have more kindness in your little finger than most people possess in their whole body. And it has power, more than you know."

"Kindness has power?" Ella asked, confused.

"And magic," her mother said. "Truly. Where there is kindness, there is goodness. And where there is goodness, there is happiness. Have courage and be kind. Will you promise?"

"I promise," Ella said, unable to stop the tears from falling.

Her mother let out a deep sigh and sank back into the pillows. "Good, good," she said. "Now I have to go, my love. Forgive me."

In that moment, Ella heard the importance in her mother's words. She did the kind thing, even though it broke her heart, and forgave her mother. For she had promised. And she would keep her word. Ella would always try to be courageous and kind.

(Oh, reader, the loss of Ella's mother was a tragedy. But do you see what I mean? Such a wonderful woman. She would have made a wonderful fairy godmother. Though I know she watches over her dear, sweet Ella, just as I do.)

Chapter Two

Six years passed, and true to her word, Ella stayed kind and courageous. She continued to make sure the smallest birds got just as much food as the big birds at the fountain. She made sure to say good morning and good evening to the cooks and maids of the house. When she had to make trips to the market, she smiled at everyone she passed. Always Ella felt her mother's presence, reminding her of the promise she had made all those years earlier.

One morning, Ella read aloud from a book in the drawing room. Her father sat in a chair opposite her, nibbling on a piece of toast slathered in honey.

Looking up, Ella smiled. She had harvested that honey especially for her father. It was his favourite treat, and the little things meant so much these days. The smile faltered a bit as she noticed the dust that had accumulated on the mantel and the curtains, which were worn thin. Since her mother's death, the house had lost some of its sparkle.

Now, now, Ella thought. *Times are not so bad. Father is here and we have a roof over our heads. And we have each other.*

With a resolved nod, she returned her attention to the book and read the final paragraph aloud: "'And thence home, and my wife and I singing, to our great content, and if ever there were a man happier in his fortunes, I know him not.'" Closing the book gently, she looked at her father. "Thus ends Mr Pepys. I do love a happy ending, don't you?"

Ella's father nodded. "They are quite my favourite sort."

"As well they should be," Ella said. She paused before adding, "I suppose it would be selfish to ask for happy beginnings and middles as well."

Silence filled the room. Both father and daughter were lost in thoughts of Mother. The book had been one of her favourites, with its grand love story and happily ever after. Many a long-ago evening had found a young Ella snuggled in her mother's lap listening to her soft breathing as she read the book.

"No," her father finally answered, breaking the silence. "I do not think that would be selfish." He paused before going on. "Ella, I have come to the conclusion that perhaps I may begin a new chapter."

Ella had been waiting for this day and knew immediately what he meant. Her father was a handsome and still rather young man. It did not make sense for him to spend the rest of his years alone. Still, her stomach fluttered uncomfortably at the thought of someone new in her life.

Ella turned her attention back to her father. "You will recall that some time ago in my travels," he was saying, "I made the acquaintance of Sir Francis Tremaine."

Ella nodded. "Yes. The master of the mercers' guild, is he not?"

"*Was*," her father corrected. "The poor man has died, alas."

"I am grieved to hear it, Father," Ella said, her voice filled with genuine sadness.

Her father looked down at his hands, which he was clenching and unclenching nervously. Then he raised his head, and his eyes met Ella's. "His widow, an honourable woman, finds herself alone, though still in the prime of her life."

Ella's gaze softened. She knew this was hard for her father to say. "You're worried about telling," she said gently. "But you mustn't.... Not if it will lead to your happiness."

"Happiness..." he repeated. "Do you think I may have another chance, even though I thought such things were done with?"

Ella did not hesitate. "I do, Father."

A relieved smile appeared over her father's face. "She would merely be your stepmother," he went on. "And you would have two lovely sisters to keep you company. So I will know, as far away as I may be, that you are safe at home, cherished and protected."

Ella knew her father had been sad, but until that moment, she hadn't realized how worried he had been, as well. Guilt flooded through her. She had promised her mother that she would be kind. The kind thing in this case would be to support her father's decision.

She stood up and hugged her father tightly. This was bound to be a big change. But perhaps there was a silver lining. She would have sisters – real sisters who could become real friends – and a stepmother, who might, in time, become like a real mother....

Within a fortnight, the plans of marriage had been made and the ceremony performed. Soon after, Ella found herself standing in front of her house waiting for the arrival of her new stepmother and stepsisters. Her father stood beside her, with a cautiously hopeful look on his face.

Ella wrung her hands. She had spent the past few days helping the staff clean the house. As Ella had looked around the home earlier that morning, she couldn't help missing her mother. Mother had loved seeing the home gleam after a fresh tidying.

The house was not the only thing to receive special attention. Ella wore her best dress, its blue complementing her eyes. Her blonde hair had been brushed until it shined and then pulled back gently. Now, standing in front of the house, she hoped that she, too, would look fine through fresh eyes.

The distinct clip-clop of hooves echoed down the drive, and within moments a carriage pulled up in front of the house. Two coachmen jumped to the ground and opened the door.

Ella's breath caught in her throat. This was it. Pasting a smile on her face, she waited for the first glimpse of her new stepmother.

Lady Tremaine's foot appeared in the door,

beautiful in an ornate shoe. A moment later, Lady Tremaine's hand appeared and took one of the coachmen's outstretched hands. Then, with practised grace, she stepped out of the carriage and onto the drive.

She was one of the most beautiful women Ella had ever seen. Her skin was radiant and soft, her strawberry-blonde hair piled atop her head in a fashionable style. Her dress, clearly the latest fashion, was pulled tight at her tiny waist, and the jewels at her throat made her eyes sparkle.

Ella's father offered his hand to his new bride. "My daughter, Ella," he said by way of introduction.

Ella curtsied. She was rewarded with a large smile from Lady Tremaine. "Please, Ella," the lady said sweetly, "let us treat each other like family." Then she motioned to the carriage. "These are your sisters, Drisella and Anastasia."

There was a small commotion and the carriage rocked gently on its wheels. Then out stepped two young ladies. The eldest, Anastasia, was pretty, with dark hair and porcelain skin.

Her sister, Drisella, had red hair and was slightly smaller in stature. Catching sight of Ella, Drisella looked her up and down, apparently not impressed. She whispered something into Anastasia's ear.

"Have courage, be kind," Ella muttered to herself. It would do no good to start off on the wrong foot. Smiling, Ella said, "How do you do? I hope you will all be happy here."

"What manners," Lady Tremaine said approvingly. She turned and gave a knowing look to her daughters.

Taking the hint, Anastasia and Drisella began to bombard Ella with hollow compliments. "You're very nice," Drisella said.

"And you have such pretty hair," said Anastasia.

Drisella nodded. "You should have it styled," she added.

The insult was not lost on Ella. Still, she refused to react. Perhaps the girls were just cranky from their journey. She continued her welcome. "Would you like a tour of the house?" Ella asked.

"What did she say?" Drisella asked her sister. "Her accent is so twangy."

"She wants to show us her farmhouse," Anastasia replied. "She's proud of it, I think."

Lady Tremaine cleared her throat, then addressed Anastasia and Drisella. "Dears," she said, her tone warning, "I do hope you won't fuss."

Her daughters snapped to attention. They were not used to being chastised by their mother. She usually let them get their way. But now she was telling them to be nice to their new country bumpkin of a sister. With a sigh, they followed Ella towards the farmhouse.

As they entered, Lady Tremaine turned to Ella's father. "You did not say that your daughter was so beautiful," she said. It had been impossible to ignore. Compared to her own daughters, Ella had a grace and beauty that made them seem dull and mindless.

"She takes after her ..." Ella's father began, but stopped himself.

Lady Tremaine finished the sentence.

"Her mother," she said, nodding. "Just so. You must not be afraid to say it. Not to me."

A relieved smile spread across his face as Lady Tremaine put a hand on his arm. But as her new husband began to give her a tour of her new home, Lady Tremaine frowned. She would have to keep an eye on Ella. The girl could prove to be trouble if she was a constant reminder to her father of the wife he had lost.

Chapter Three

A short while later, the new family members made their way into the drawing room.

"How long has your family lived here?" Drisella asked, running a finger along the fireplace mantel and checking it for dust.

"Over 200 years," Ella's father replied quite proudly.

Anastasia snorted. "And in all that time, they never thought to decorate?"

"Hush," Lady Tremaine snapped. "They will think you are serious."

Ella's father, however, stared at his new wife,

trying to gauge *her* feelings about the place. "Well?" he asked, hoping for her approval.

Lady Tremaine looked around the room, her gaze flitting from the chairs to the pictures on the wall. In turn, Ella watched Lady Tremaine. She knew that the woman was judging the house and, therefore, her mother's touch. Finally, Lady Tremaine answered, "Very homely." While her smile seemed approving, Ella couldn't help noting the double meanings of the word. Her stepmother went on. "It does lack a little sparkle and gaiety. Though I suppose there has been little enough to celebrate ... until now. We must change that!"

As she spoke, Lady Tremaine looked directly at Ella. If Ella were to disagree, it would seem rude, and Ella knew her father would be hurt. So she simply nodded. While she liked the house, it might not be such a bad idea to bring some life back into the place, add a little more laughter. What harm could come from that?

Lady Tremaine wasted no time in planning many parties. She invited everyone she thought worthy, including numerous well-dressed lords and ladies. The household staff found themselves stuffed into formal servants' outfits while the cook baked and grilled and baked some more. As the guests began to arrive, the house did indeed fill with laughter. But, Ella noted as she looked around the room, the laughter was not kind. It was snide.

Ella watched as her stepmother and her guests speculated on the goings-on in the kingdom, cackling meanly as they gossiped. Then, noticing movement out of the corner of her eye, Ella glanced to the side of the room. She smiled as she saw a tiny house mouse, whom she had named Jacqueline, making off with a fallen chunk of cheese. The food was nearly as big as the mouse herself, and she struggled under its weight.

Suddenly, Ella heard a hiss. Lady Tremaine's beloved cat, Lucifer, was stalking over. The name fit the creature perfectly. He was the one animal Ella had not been able to win over.

He was mean and aloof, showing affection only to Lady Tremaine and snapping at anyone else who dared to come near him.

"Just what do you think you're up to, Lucifer?" Ella asked, reaching down and picking up the cat by the scruff of his neck. "Jacqueline is my guest. And the eating of guests is not allowed." Nodding at the little mouse, Ella took Lucifer out of the room.

Enough had changed already in her home. The least she could do was make sure her old friends were safe from the new intruders – even if she wasn't so lucky.

Down the hall, Ella's father sat in his study, going over his accounts. Ella stood in the doorway, looking around the familiar room. The same worn chair sat in the corner, a quilt thrown over its back. Books collected over years of travel lined the shelves. An oversized desk dominated the space, every inch covered by papers.

Lady Tremaine's touch had not found its way to this room, and for that, Ella was glad. She had spent countless hours cuddled up on the chair reading, while her father worked. It was a peaceful space and now a source of refuge.

"You're missing the party," Ella said, walking into the study.

Ella's father looked up and smiled wearily. "I imagine it is much like all the others. And I'm leaving first thing."

"You're hardly back from the last trip," Ella said, her voice quavering. "Do you have to go?"

"I'm afraid so," her father replied. He gestured at the piles of papers. "With a larger household, more bills. I must provide for you all, even if it means a little travel."

"I do not need much," Ella said softly, though she knew it was not for her that he needed the money. Her new stepsisters and stepmother were used to a certain quality of life, one that was very different from Ella's. Yet they were now a family, and as such, Ella reminded herself, they would have to learn to live together. It was what Mother would have wanted. Realizing that her mind had been elsewhere, Ella shook her head. "I'll pack your quinine against scurvy," she informed her father. "And your Warburg's Physic for the seasickness."

Her father gave her a warm smile. "Capital," he said. "And what would you like me to bring you home from abroad? Your sisters...." His voice trailed off as Ella shot him a pointed look. He cleared his throat and corrected himself. "Your *step*sisters have asked me for parasols and lace. What will you have?"

"Nothing, Father," Ella replied. *Of course they would ask for such things when it is their already high demands that cause Father to travel,* she added silently.

" 'Nothing will come of nothing', " her father replied, smiling mischievously.

Ella returned the smile. This was one of the games they played: identify the quote. When she was younger, the quotes had been simple, but now her father enjoyed testing her with more obscure references. This one, however, she knew. *"King Lear."* Her father nodded proudly. Suddenly, inspiration struck. "I know," she said. "Bring me the first branch your shoulder brushes on your journey."

Her father cocked his head. "That is a curious request."

"You'll have to take it with you on your way," Ella explained, "and think of me when you look at it. And when you bring it back, it means that you will be with it." Her face grew serious as she looked at her father. He seemed smaller to her, weaker even. She knew that each trip he made took a toll on him. "And that's what I really want – for you to come back. No matter what." She shuddered as a wave of foreboding washed over her. She had a terrible feeling, as if her father wasn't coming home.

"I will," Ella's father replied. He paused and then added, "Now, Ella, while I'm away, you must be good to your stepmother and stepsisters. Even though they may be ... trying at times."

"I promise," Ella replied.

"Thank you," her father said, sounding relieved. "I always leave a part of me behind, Ella. Remember that. And your mother is here, too, though you see her not. She is the very heart of this place. That is why we must cherish this house, always. For her."

Ella's throat closed up. They very rarely spoke of Mother these days. "I miss her," Ella said softly. "Do you?"

"Very much," her father said. "Very much."

As Ella and her father fell into companionable silence, they were unaware of a figure just outside the door. Lady Tremaine had heard them talking of Ella's mother and felt a wave of anger and jealousy rush over her. Her new husband's words just then felt like a betrayal.

Shaking her head, Lady Tremaine turned and walked back down the hall. It was pointless to allow emotion to get the better of her. She was the lady of the house now, and she would make sure Ella learned that while her father was away.

All too soon, Ella once again found herself standing in front of the house looking at a carriage. But this time the carriage was not bringing a new family home to her; it was taking her only real family away. As her father waved goodbye, Ella's eyes filled with tears. Lady Tremaine stood beside her, her back straight and her expression unreadable.

Anastasia and Drisella were less upset. "Remember the lace," Anastasia called.

"And my parasol!" Drisella added. "For my complexion!" With that, the Tremaines headed inside, leaving Ella alone.

When the carriage was finally out of sight, Ella also made her way back into the house. She was passing the drawing room when she heard her name called. Wiping tears from her eyes, she entered the room.

Lady Tremaine was seated comfortably on one of the chaise-longues. Her hands were clasped in her lap, and a look of smug pleasure spread over her face. From down the hall, Ella could hear her stepsisters arguing about clothes and wardrobe space. "Yes, Stepmother?"

Lady Tremaine smiled coldly. "You needn't call me that," she replied. "Madam will do." She paused as one of her daughters let out a piercing shriek. Then she went on.

"Anastasia and Drisella have always shared a room. Such dear, affectionate girls. I think they are finding the quarters rather confining."

Ella listened to the screaming from the hall. She couldn't argue with her stepmother. Her new sisters did seem on edge. And she had made a promise to her father to make them feel welcome. "My bedroom is the biggest besides yours and Father's. Perhaps they would like to have it?"

Lady Tremaine raised an eyebrow. She had expected to *tell* Ella to give up her room, not have it offered.

"I can stay in …" Ella went on.

"The attic," her stepmother finished. "Quite so."

Ella was taken aback. *The attic?*

"It's nice and airy," Lady Tremaine went on. "And you shall be away from all our fuss and bother. It would be even more cosy for you if you kept all of this…." Her hand swept around the room, indicating the small objects and keepsakes Ella and her father had collected over the years. Lady Tremaine's hand paused on a small portrait of Ella's mother before she finished. "... bric-a-brac up there with you. To keep you amused."

Ella was quiet as she glanced at the 'bric-a-brac'. Her eyes landed on the image of her mother. *Have courage and be kind. Promise me.* Her mother's last words to her echoed through Ella's head. A protest died on her lips and she simply nodded. "Madam."

Lady Tremaine smiled as though she had won a great battle. And then she pointed to the books on the shelves. "You may take these away as well," she said. "Natural philosophy, mathematics, histories? These books are too ... bookish for me. They depress my spirits. And they take up space."

Lady Tremaine stood up, grabbed one of the books, and handed it to Ella. Ella nearly gasped aloud. There, sparkling on the ring finger of Lady Tremaine's left hand, was the engagement ring Ella's father had given to her mother. Why was Lady Tremaine wearing it? Ella knew her father would never have given it to her.

Ella didn't know what to say or do. She was

overwhelmed by the sight of her stepmother wearing her mother's ring, and her new living arrangements. Without her father's reassuring presence, she had no one to turn to for comfort or guidance.

Stopping to collect a few things from her old room, she made her way up to the attic. When she opened the door, she was met with a gust of cold, dusty air. No one had been up there in years, and cobwebs hung from the ceiling, while a thick layer of dust coated the floor. Various objects were strewn about, having been dumped into the attic when they were no longer of use. *Just like me,* Ella thought. She spotted a narrow, old bed in the corner and moved it under the single window. Then she sat down. "Well," she said aloud, trying to make the best of it, "no one shall disturb me here."

As if on cue, Ella heard a tiny squeak. Then she saw Jacqueline and Gus, the two house mice. "Oh!" she cried out, pleased to see her friends. "So this is where you take refuge. Me too, it would seem."

The small, furry creatures looked up at her, their little whiskers wiggling as though in agreement.

Ella smiled. Perhaps this wouldn't be so bad after all. There were no stepmothers, step-sisters, or even troublesome stepcats to bother her and her animal companions. No, this might not be so bad at all. Plus, now that she had been sentenced to the attic, things couldn't possibly get any worse, could they?

Ella quickly discovered that things could, indeed, get worse. She was at the mercy of her new family's every whim. They complained that the country air exhausted them, so, in order to help the staff with the Tremaines' increasing demands, Ella began taking breakfast to their rooms every morning. Soon their lethargy started to extend through supper, tea and dinner as well. The bells in the kitchen that had long been covered by dust through lack of use began to ring throughout the day, signalling yet more requests from Ella's stepfamily.

While Anastasia and Drisella lounged, Ella rushed to and fro, picking up empty plates and clearing the dirty laundry only to watch her sisters carelessly throw more clothes on the ground. When the girls and their mother retired to the drawing room for the afternoon, Ella was expected to make sure the dust was wiped clear and the curtains were pulled back to let in the sun. There was always a complaint. A smidge of dust, the sun too bright.

One afternoon, as Ella moved around the drawing room, Drisella practised her singing and Anastasia drew. Neither girl was good at her hobby, and while Ella tried not to, she couldn't help cringing when Drisella hit a particularly high note.

Perched in her chair, Lady Tremaine watched her stepdaughter rush to and fro. Despite her dirty dress and her messy hair, she was still infinitely more poised than either of Lady Tremaine's daughters. She did what she was asked, always agreeably, always willingly, and it infuriated Lady Tremaine. The lady realized that if she wanted her daughters to look better, she would simply have to make Ella look worse. She would have to figure out a way to extinguish the light of Ella's good character – at any cost.

(Oh, dear reader, can you see how dark hearts are so scared of the light? Always so cruel, these jealous types. Funny how they never seem to learn....)

Chapter Four

The days blurred one into another, with Ella the constant victim of her stepmother's increasing demands. The only things that kept her going were her father's letters and the thought of her father's eventual return. And then, one afternoon, she heard the familiar clop of hoofbeats outside and then a loud knock at the door.

"At last!" Ella cried, racing down the stairs.

As she flung open the door, the smile on her face faltered, replaced with a confused expression. A farmer stood in the doorway. He held his hat in one hand. In his other hand, he held the reins of Galahad's bridle. The big horse's head hung low, the cart behind him empty. Her father was nowhere to be seen.

The farmer looked at the ground and then slowly back up, his eyes sad. "It's your father, miss. He took ill on the road. He's passed on, miss. He's gone."

This was too much to bear. Ella's vision began to blur and the blood drained from her face, leaving her pale and shaking. She reached out a hand and clutched the doorframe for support. Behind her, Lady Tremaine, Anastasia and Drisella appeared.

The farmer looked crestfallen. "To the end, he spoke of no one but you, miss," he said, trying to help. "And your mother."

Lady Tremaine's mouth narrowed.

Unaware of the impact of his words, the farmer went on. "I was to give you this." Reaching into a bag at his side, he pulled out a dried branch.

Tears welled in her eyes as Ella gingerly took the branch and held it to her heart. Behind her, Anastasia and Drisella began to whine.

"But what about my lace?" Anastasia asked. "And my parasol," Drisella added.

"Can't you see?" Lady Tremaine snapped. "None of that matters."

Ella met her stepmother's gaze. A flicker of compassion stirred deep inside. *Can it be?* she thought. Did her stepmother share her sorrow? But then Lady Tremaine spoke again.

"We're ruined," she said. "How will we live?" She ushered her daughters away. Behind her, Ella thanked the farmer and slowly shut the door. When no one was looking, she collapsed against it, her heart broken. She was well and truly alone. And she couldn't help wondering, what would happen to her now?

Ella didn't have to wait long to find out her fate. Within days of receiving news of Ella's father's death, Lady Tremaine let the household staff go. With them gone, and her stepmother apparently too weak with grief to do anything, the duties of the house now fell fully on Ella's shoulders. It was left to her to pack up her father's clothes and sell them for whatever meagre price they would fetch. When her sisters required their daily baths, it was Ella who made her way to the well and fetched buckets of water, then carried them slowly back to the house.

Anyone else might have buckled under the added burdens, but no matter what task Lady Tremaine or her stepsisters threw at her, Ella focused on staying positive. She hummed while she picked vegetables from the greenhouse. She sang as she washed and ironed. She even smiled as she helped Lady Tremaine into her dresses that cost more than the fired staff.

She saw how her stepmother looked at her – as just another mouth to feed, an interloper in the house that now belonged to her. But Ella had made promises – the one years earlier to her mother and the more recent one to her father. And she would not break those promises. Even if, as the days passed, she became less a sister and daughter and more a servant.

At night, after the last of her chores was done and her stepmother and sisters were tucked into their beds, Ella was finally able to rest.

Only then would her humming end, and she would let some sadness creep into her heart.

One night, after a particularly long day, she found herself too exhausted to eat. Putting the small chunk of bread and meagre serving of cheese on the floor, she called out to her only friends – the mice, Jacqueline and Gus. They appeared quickly, followed by their two small children, whom Ella had named Esau and Jacob. She watched as they ate their dinner. Ella was happy to see someone enjoying it.

And then, too tired to walk up the stairs to the attic, she curled up in a ball on the hearth of the fireplace and fell asleep, the dying embers providing at least a little heat for her chilled and aching bones....

Ella woke with a start. The embers in the fireplace had long since grown cold, and she could hear her stepsisters and stepmother rustling about upstairs. Panicked, she leaped to her feet and scrambled around the kitchen, putting breakfast together. As the water began to boil, she rang the bell indicating breakfast was ready. The Tremaines had been taking their meals downstairs as of late, and they expected breakfast at the same time every morning.

A few minutes later, Ella entered the drawing room to stoke the fire. Her stepfamily had already arrived, and she was greeted with a cold stare from Lady Tremaine.

"I thought breakfast was ready," she said, her mouth turning down at the corners.

"It is, madam," Ella answered. "I am only mending the fire."

This reply did not seem to ease Lady Tremaine's anger. "In the future," she snapped, "can we not be called until the work is done?"

Ella nodded. "As you wish." She went to retrieve the eggs and tea and then quickly returned. As she began to serve, Lady Tremaine raised an eyebrow.

"What is that on your face?" she asked.

Ella lifted a hand and gently wiped it across her cheek. Her fingers, when she looked at them, were covered in a fine layer of black soot.

"It's ash from the fireplace!" Anastasia exclaimed, laughing out loud. Drisella quickly joined in.

"Clean yourself up," Lady Tremaine said. "You'll get cinders in our tea." While her tone was disapproving, Ella couldn't help noticing that her stepmother seemed pleased to see her in such a state. And her stepsisters were clearly thrilled.

Drisella bounced in her seat, clapping her hands in glee. "I've got a new name for her!" she cried. "Cinderwench!"

Anastasia looked Ella up and down. "I couldn't bear to look so dirty." Then, smiling cruelly, she added, "Dirty Ella."

"Cinderella!" Drisella exclaimed. "That's what we'll call you."

As her stepsisters continued to tease her, Ella tried to ignore them and serve breakfast. When her stepfamily had their food, she moved to her seat at the table. Until then, this had been the only meal she was still able to share with her 'family'. But Lady Tremaine's voice stopped her.

"Who's this for?" she asked, pointing at Ella's plate. "Is there someone we've forgotten?"

"It is my place," Ella said.

Lady Tremaine shook her head. "It just seems too much to expect you to prepare breakfast, serve it and still sit with us. Wouldn't you prefer to eat when all the work is done, Ella? Or, should I say, Cinderella?"

For a moment, Ella said nothing. Her stepsisters looked on as if waiting for her to oppose their mother. But instead, Ella simply nodded and said, "If you please, madam." Then, picking up her plate, she left the room.

It was only when she was safely in the kitchen that tears filled Ella's eyes. Then her hands began to shake violently, causing her to drop her plate. It fell to the floor and shattered, causing Ella's tears to fall faster.

Kneeling, she began to pick up the pieces. Ella caught sight of her reflection in the copper pot hanging from the hearth and gasped. Her face was indeed covered in ashes and her blonde hair was tangled and unruly. She *was* Cinderella.

Suddenly, something inside Ella broke. For so long she had been trying to be the girl her mother and father would be proud of. She had kept her promises and tried to be gentle and kind. She had been courageous in the face of many unknowns and stayed strong when left alone. But now it seemed all for naught. Her new 'family' had turned her into a creature of ash and toil. She was nothing but their plaything, someone to mock and order about. It was all too much.

Jumping to her feet, Ella threw off her apron, and she raced for the stable. Luckily, Lady Tremaine had seen the worth in keeping a horse on the property, so Galahad remained, happily munching hay in his stall. Hearing her footsteps, he lifted his big grey head. A moment later, Ella had him in the aisle and was pulling herself up onto his strong back. Before anyone could stop her, she urged the horse forward and they took off.

The trees whipped by in a blur and the wind prickled Ella's eyes, but she didn't care. Beneath her, Galahad's strong stride was calming and reassuring, a reminder of days gone by when she would ride for hours around the meadow, her father teaching her how to post, pick up the proper lead and, eventually, take small jumps.

Now, immersed in the fresh air, Ella felt like she could breathe for the first time in a long while. As they continued to race along, a smile spread across her face.

And then, right in front of them, a stag leaped out of the woods.

Galahad reared back, spooked, almost throwing Ella to the ground. Her legs gripped the horse's sides and she stayed astride. When she was sure Galahad wouldn't rear again, she began to rub his neck, calming him. It was only then that she noticed the sounds of an approaching hunt: the baying of hounds, along with the shouts of men and the pounding of horses' hooves. Ella knew that if the hunt caught up with this beautiful creature, he would be killed. She couldn't let that happen. "Run!" she called to the stag. "Go! Quickly!"

As if he understood, the stag bolted into the trees, disappearing into the thick brush. Moments later, the ground beneath Galahad shook and the forest exploded with the sounds of the hunters, who seemed to be very nearby now. Spooked once more, Galahad started to gallop as fast as he could. Ella tried to slow him, pulling the reins and calling to him.

Suddenly, another rider appeared beside them, pulling at Galahad's reins and slowing him to a trot. Ella patted Galahad's mane, eager to make sure Galahad was okay.

Then she found herself peering up at the other horse. A tall, athletic horse. And on the tall horse's back, peering at her with an amused expression on his face, was the most handsome man she had ever seen.

Chapter Five

*T*he prince let out a sigh. He was tired of the endless hunts. The pageantry of it all ... the racing endlessly through the forest after a helpless beast that had done nothing to deserve its fate. Yet he was the prince.

The day's hunt had started out like any other. The baying of the hounds as the horn was blown. The initial rush he felt as the throng of horses took off, their heads pulling at the bits in their eagerness. But after that, the prince had felt nothing. He galloped along, his head a million miles away, as men whooped and hollered around him. The chase took them deep into the kingdom's forest, and after a while, the prince couldn't tell one grove of trees from another. The hounds grew more anxious as the smell of the stag grew stronger. There was a flash of movement through the trees, and the prince knew the end was near.

And then there was chaos.

The horses whinnied as they suddenly switched directions. The prince spotted a different horse across the way, one that was sprinting haphazardly and was dangerously close to throwing its rider.

Quickly guiding his horse towards it, the prince reached out and grabbed the reins, pulling with all his might. The two horses slowed and started to circle each other. It was then that the prince got a good look at the girl astride the other horse. Her hair was tangled about her face, and her dress was mottled with mud. But when she looked at him, her eyes were unafraid. For a moment, he was lost in their depths, seeing sadness behind the courage.

"Are you all right?" he asked.

"I'm all right. But you've nearly frightened the life out of him," the girl replied.

Her answer surprised him and the prince cocked an eyebrow. "Who?"

"The stag," the girl said matter-of-factly. "What has he ever done to you that you should chase him about?"

The prince stifled a smile. It was amusing to hear his own thoughts echoed back to him aloud. "I confess I have never met him before. Is he a friend of yours?"

"An acquaintance," she answered. "We met just now. I looked into his eyes, and he looked into mine, and I felt he had a great deal left to do with his life. That's all."

For a moment, the prince was struck silent. He had never met a girl like this before. He was used to folks falling all over themselves to say whatever they thought would please him. But this girl? She was the most forthright person he had ever met. And he wanted to know more about her.

"What do they call you?" he asked.

To his surprise, the girl blushed, as though the question made her uncomfortable. "Never mind what they call me," she said.

The prince watched as she began to check her horse, clearly anxious to make sure he was all right. She seemed undaunted by the forest around her and the strange man in front of her. "You shouldn't be this deep in the forest alone," the prince said, trying not to stare at her hair, turned golden by the sun.

"I'm not alone," the girl said, shrugging. "I'm with you." Then she paused. "What do they call you?"

The question brought the prince up short. Clearly she didn't know who he was, and he didn't want to spoil the moment by revealing his true identity. He racked his brain, unsure what to say. Finally, he decided to tell her a part truth. "They call me Kit," he said. It was his childhood nickname, used by his father.

The girl nodded. "Where do you live, Mr Kit?" she asked.

"I, uh, live at the palace," he stammered. "My father is teaching me his trade."

Again, it wasn't exactly a lie. He *did* live at the palace, though his 'trade' was not traditional.

"You're an apprentice?" the girl asked. "That is very fine. Do they treat you well?"

Kit was beginning to feel slightly guilty. He didn't want to lie to her, but this was one of the most interesting conversations he had had in a while. That would change if she found out he was royalty. "Better than I deserve, most likely," he finally answered. Then, trying to change the subject, he asked, "And you?"

A look of sadness flashed across the girl's face. "They treat me as well as they are able," she said.

"I'm sorry," Kit said, his voice gentle. For some reason, the sadness in her eyes made him angry. He wanted to find out who would cause such a look in a girl who seemed so strong.

"It's not your doing," the girl replied. Then she straightened her shoulders and her eyes grew bright again. "It's not so very bad. Others have it worse, I'm sure. We must simply have courage and be kind, mustn't we?"

Kit was taken aback. "Yes, you're right." It was a simple notion, but the girl said it with such conviction. It echoed his own feelings, and he felt himself on the verge of saying so. But then the sound of a horn echoed through the forest.

The girl looked panicked. "Please don't let them hurt him!" she shouted.

"But ... we're hunting," Kit explained. "It's what's done."

"Just because it's what's done doesn't mean it's what *should* be done," the girl said. "Leave him alone, won't you?"

Kit started to argue, but then he shook his head. No, the girl was right. There was no reason for the hunt. "All right," he agreed, and smiled.

She returned his smile. "Thank you very much, Mr Kit," she said.

Another peal of the hunting horn blasted through the woods, and at the edge of the clearing a man on horseback appeared. Kit stifled a groan. This was his captain of the guard, and he was obviously not pleased the prince had slipped his watch.

"Your High –" the Captain began.

The prince quickly interrupted him. "It's me, *Kit*. I'm Kit," he said, his meaning clear. "And I'm on my way."

An amused expression crossed the Captain's face, but he left it at that. Kit met the girl's gaze. "I hope that I will see you again," he said.

"And I, you," she replied.

Before either of them could say anything else, the horn gave another frantic blast, and Kit turned his horse. As he galloped away, he sneaked one last look over his shoulder. The girl stood there, holding her horse's reins in one hand, the other raised in a wave goodbye. As she disappeared from sight, Kit felt a funny sadness fill his chest. She was the most interesting girl he had ever met. What if he never got to see her again?

The next day Kit stood in his father's bedroom, waiting as the royal physician finished his examination of the king. The older man stood there, clearly annoyed by a process that was becoming all too familiar. Finally, the visit over, Kit helped his father back into his tunic and then began to lead him towards a chair. But his father shooed him away and deliberately continued to stand.

"You sound as if you're the first fellow who ever met a pretty girl," King Frederick said, continuing their earlier conversation. Ever since Kit had arrived home from the previous day's hunt, he had talked of nothing but this mysterious girl in the woods.

Kit let out a sigh. "She wasn't a pretty girl," he retorted. Then he corrected himself. "Well, she was a pretty girl. But there was so much more to her."

"How much more?" King Frederick asked. "You've only met her once. How can you know anything about her?"

Kit had a quick answer for that. "You told me you knew right away when you met Mother."

The king groaned. His son was as stubborn as he had been at that age. "That's different," he snapped. "Your mother was a princess."

"You would have loved her anyway," Kit replied. That was true. His mother and father had had a grand love.

But his father shook his head. "I would never have met her, because it wouldn't have been appropriate. And *my* father, rest his bones, would have told me what I'm telling you. And *I* would have listened."

Kit smiled. "No, you wouldn't." Then he turned to the doctor, who had been quietly packing up his tools and trying hard not to listen in on the conversation. "How is he?"

The doctor took a moment, as though trying to figure out the best way to deliver the news. The pause spoke volumes, and the king raised a hand, stopping him. "Never mind. If it takes that long to work out a way to say it, I already know it's bad."

"Father," Kit began, all earlier thoughts of teasing evaporated.

The king simply shook his head. "It's the way of all flesh, boy. Come. We will be late. And punctuality is the politeness of princes."

Kit sighed. There was no sense in arguing

with his father when his mind was set. So he helped the older man into his jacket, and together they strode out of the room.

In the corridor they were joined by two men – the Grand Duke and the Captain of the Guard. While the Captain was tall and muscular, the Grand Duke was short and round. Despite their physical differences, the two men had two common goals – to keep the king and prince safe and to look after the well-being of the kingdom. How they did so differed, however. The Grand Duke followed the letter of the law to a tee; the Captain was a bit more lax, making him Kit's ally on more than one occasion.

"My King," the Grand Duke said as the men started walking down the corridor. He narrowed his gaze at Kit. "Your Highness. I am sure your father spoke to you of your behaviour in the forest?"

"Is it any business of yours, Grand Duke?" Kit replied.

The Grand Duke puffed out his chest. "Your business is my business, Your Highness," he said, sounding miffed. "It will not do to let the stag go free."

A flash of blue eyes and blonde hair popped into Kit's mind, and he found himself echoing the girl's words. "Just because it's what's done doesn't mean it's what *should* be done." The three older men stopped and stared at him. Kit shrugged. "Or something like that."

The group resumed their walk. "Still the dreamer," King Frederick said, trying not to smile. While he would never admit it out loud, he remembered what it felt like to be young and optimistic. "I had hoped that a bit of campaigning would knock some sense into you." He turned and addressed the Captain. "What have you got to say?"

The Captain was an experienced soldier who had fought alongside the prince in many a battle. "I'd say the war knocked some common sense *out* of him, sir. While I have never seen a fellow more brave, he exhibited a very troublesome tendency to ... think."

"Sometimes I fear for this kingdom," King

Frederick replied, not sure whether the Captain meant his comment as a good or bad thing.

Silence fell over the group as they left the grand hall and entered one of the palace's many salons. An artist was setting up his paints. Upon their entrance, he bowed low.

"Make him look marriageable, Master Phineas," the king ordered the portraitist, causing Kit to groan. "We must attract a suitable bride, even if he is a terrible dunce."

"I shall endeavour to please, Your Highness," the artist replied seriously. Then, taking a quick look at Kit, who was doing his best to look awkward and very *un*marriageable, he added under his breath, "But I can't work miracles." He turned back to a large canvas that stretched at least three metres into the air. Already the beginnings of the portrait could be seen – the prince, astride a beautiful horse, holding a sword high in his hand as though to say, "Onward!" The only thing left to do was the face – if Kit would cooperate.

The prince begrudgingly climbed onto a

saddle on a sawhorse. "So these portraits will be sent abroad?" he asked out of the corner of his mouth.

"Yes," King Frederick replied. "If we can convince a princess of sufficient rank that you are not a dunderhead, we may be able to secure a powerful alliance."

Kit started to laugh but a stern look from the artist stopped him. "At this ball you and the Grand Duke insist upon?" The ball had been the topic of discussion for far too long in his opinion.

"At which you will choose a bride," the king said. Kit shot him a look, and King Frederick went on, his voice stern. "It has always been done; it is how it *will* be done."

"We are a small kingdom among great states, Your Highness," the Grand Duke added. "And it is a dangerous world. We must get what allies we can."

Sitting on his fake horse, Kit wanted to scream. He had been born into this life. He had not asked for it, and now he felt as though he were a prized pig being fattened up to sell at market. He knew he was lucky in many ways. But the freedom of the girl in the woods? That was something he could never have.

"If I must marry," the prince said aloud, "why could I not wed, say ... a good, honest country girl?"

The Grand Duke scoffed. "How many divisions of infantry would this 'good, honest country girl' provide us?"

Taking a gentler tone, the king tried to make the point clear. "You will be king soon, Son. You know I am not well." The others began to protest but he hushed them and went on. "For myself, I do not mind. I have had a good life. But I would have you – and the kingdom – safe and secure."

Kit felt a wave of remorse for being so stubborn. His father *was* ill and he meant well. Suddenly, Kit had an idea. Perhaps there was a way to appease his father and get a chance to see the girl from the woods again. He knew that if his father met her, he would see why Kit was so intrigued. "All right, I will agree to the ball." The Grand Duke began to clap, but Kit went on. "On one condition. The invitations go to everyone, not just the nobility. The wars have brought sorrow enough." He looked at his father. "If you were in my place, you would do the same."

The king shook his head. "But I don't want to do what *I* would in *your* place. I want *you* to do what I, in *my* place, tell you, in *your* place, to do." Realizing that he was making no sense, the king threw his hands up in the air.

The Grand Duke, however, seemed pleased with the outcome. "I think we may have struck a bargain," he said. "A ball for the people, a princess for the prince."

In his saddle, Kit tried not to smile too broadly. True, it wasn't ideal. He would have to meet many girls in whom he had no interest. But with luck, his mystery girl from the woods would be at the ball. And with even greater luck, he would have the chance to get lost in her blue eyes once more. And maybe, just maybe, he'd find a way to convince his father that some traditions were meant to be broken.

Chapter Six

The market was bustling. At several stands, grocers called out their wares, advertising the freshest vegetables, the plumpest fruits. A handsome florist held out a bouquet of bright daisies to a group of girls, causing them to giggle and avert their eyes. At the end of the market, away from the more pleasant smells, the fishmonger put out the day's catch.

In the midst of it all was Ella, a basket in one hand, a dreamy look on her face. Ever since her encounter with Kit, she had felt as though she were floating. She knew it was silly. Chances were she'd never see him again. But for that one moment, there in the woods, she had felt as though Kit had seen her for who she was, not as the girl of ashes her stepfamily had turned her into.

"If it isn't Miss Ella." Flora, the household's cook, strode up to her, smiling warmly.

"Flora!" Ella pulled her into an embrace. "Are you well? Have you found employment?"

"Can anyone roast a chicken better, I ask you?" Flora and Ella laughed together. But then Flora's head cocked and a look of concern crossed her face. "You don't look well, miss, not at all."

Ella wiped at her face and tucked an unruly piece of hair behind her ear. She looked down at her tattered, threadbare dress and sighed. Flora wasn't wrong.

Flora put a hand on Ella's shoulder. "Why do you stay there, when they treat you so?"

Ella smiled and shrugged. "I made Mother and Father a promise to cherish the place where we were so happy. They loved our house, and now that they are gone, I love it for them. So it's my home, you see."

Nearby, an old beggar woman lifted her head, listening to Ella with interest. She smiled and then turned at the sound of a loud commotion from the middle of the square.

(Aha! I would remember this poor soul, gentle reader. For sometimes the people most overlooked are the ones who turn out to be most surprising....)

Ella, too, looked towards the square and raised an eyebrow at the sight of the royal crier holding a large scroll. He stood on the edge of the town fountain, waiting for the people to gather. Curious, Ella moved closer and waited for his announcement.

"Hear ye! Hear ye!" the man cried, silencing the crowd. "Know that our good King Frederick, fourth of that name; Protector of the Realm; Holy Elector of Thuringia; Sire of the Imperial Purple; Earl of Lambert, Chataway and Moggan; Companion of the Path of Honour...." The crier's voice trailed off and he took a deep breath. Then he went on. "Defender of the Faithful; and Scourge of the Heretic, has decided to honour the safe return from the wars of his son...." Once again, the crier took a deep breath, and the crowd began to groan at the thought of another long list of titles. But they all felt quite relieved when the crier simply said, "The prince. On this day, two weeks hence, there shall be held, at the palace, a royal ball."

There was silence at the news. After all, what did a royal ball have to do with any of them? They were commoners. They did not dance or attend balls.

The crier went on. "At said ball, in accordance with ancient custom, the prince shall choose a bride." And then, with great pomp and circumstance, the crier finished his announcement. "Furthermore, at the behest of the prince, it is hereby declared that every maiden in the kingdom, be she noble or commoner, is invited to attend."

As all around her people began to chat excitedly with one another, Ella was silent. But her heart pounded loudly in her ears. A ball? At the palace? And she could attend? That meant she would have a chance to see Kit again!

After all, he was an apprentice at the palace! A huge smile spread across her face.

When she arrived home, Ella shared the news. Instantly, her stepsisters began to chatter excitedly. It was clear they had lofty goals – namely, the prince's hand in marriage.

"I shall trick him into loving me," Drisella said, twirling around the drawing room. "See if I don't!"

"This is the most hugeous news!" Anastasia exclaimed excitedly.

Lady Tremaine stood in the middle of the room, watching her daughters with a critical eye. "Calm yourselves," she finally said. "Listen to me." It took several moments, but finally Anastasia and Drisella focused. Satisfied she had their attention, Lady Tremaine went on. "One of you *must* win the heart of the prince. Do that, and we can unwind the debt in which we were ensnared when we came to this backwater." She turned and narrowed her eyes at Ella, who was standing quietly in the corner, lost in her own thoughts. "Having delivered your news, why are you still here? You must return to town right away and tell that seamstress to run us up three fine ball gowns."

"Three?" Ella repeated, surprised. She hadn't expected her stepmother to provide her with a dress. Collecting herself, Ella said, "That is ... very thoughtful of you."

Lady Tremaine raised an eyebrow. "What do you mean?"

"To think of me," Ella replied.

"Think of you?" Lady Tremaine repeated, sounding confused.

On the other side of the room, Drisella let out a cruel laugh. "Mummy!" she cried. "She believes the other dress is for *her*!" There was a beat as the two sisters and their mother exchanged bemused expressions. "Poor, slow little Cinders. How embarrassing!"

Lady Tremaine shook her head. "You are too ambitious for your own good."

"But I only want to see my friend," Ella protested. She should have known. Why would her stepmother choose now to show kindness?

Lady Tremaine went on. "Let me be very clear. One gown for Drisella, one for Anastasia and one for me. *À la mode Parisienne.*"

"She doesn't know what that means," Anastasia said glibly.

To their surprise, Ella lifted her head high and pulled her shoulders back, every inch the composed lady. *"Mais bien sûr je connais la mode Parisienne et je vais faire mon meilleure à le démissioner,"* she replied in fluent French.

Ella stifled a smile as she watched her stepmother and stepsisters gape at her. They had clearly not expected her to be able to speak French, much less so well. Recovering, Lady Tremaine clapped her hands. "Right. That's settled, then. Now go! Every bit of baggage in the kingdom will be tilting at the prince. You must get there first, before the seamstress is drowning in work." Without another word, she turned her back, dismissing Ella.

Ella left the drawing room. She knew she shouldn't have shown off like that, but it had felt nice to catch her stepfamily off guard.

And the joke was on them, anyway, because she had never expected a dress; she knew what she could wear. Plus, she had no desire to become a princess. All she wanted was to see Kit and have an evening during which she could be just a girl enjoying the company of a nice boy.

Inside a large palace room, the prince's regiment trained. The sound of clanging metal echoed through the large space. In the centre of it all, Kit parried back and forth with the Captain of the Guard. While his movements were clean and precise, he was distracted. Noticing his pupil's lack of concentration, the Captain struck with his sword, rapping the prince sharply on his arm.

"Wake up, Your Highness," he said. "You're in a daze."

Kit looked guiltily at the Captain. "I'm sorry," he said. Then he thrust his own sword forward, forcing the Captain into a duel.

As they moved back and forth across the room, they slung not only swords, but words as well. "You've been off since the hunt," the Captain said, bringing down his sword and just missing Kit.

"It's the girl," the prince replied, taking a few quick steps forward and pushing the Captain back. "I've never met anyone like her."

"There are plenty of other girls," the Captain replied.

Kit shook his head, his sword faltering. "But her spirit," he countered. "Her *goodness*...."

"I don't suppose she has a sister," the Captain said, raising his sword to indicate a time-out. He had to admit that from the way Kit spoke of this girl, she seemed the picture of perfection. "I don't know," Kit said, shrugging. "I don't know anything about her."

"Well, perhaps your mystery girl will come to the ball. That is why you threw the doors open, is it not?"

Kit looked at him and feigned indignation. "Captain," he said as though wounded. "It was for the benefit of the *people*."

"Of course," the Captain said, hiding a smile. "How shallow of me. And if she comes? Then you will tell her that you are the prince?

And the prince may choose whatever bride he wants?"

The prince let out a bitter laugh. "You know my father and the Grand Duke will only have me marry a princess."

"If this girl from the forest is as charming as you say, they may change their minds," the Captain suggested.

Kit shook his head. "Father *might* understand," he conceded. "But the Grand Duke? Never."

As the sounds of swordplay swelled around them, the two men grew silent. The Captain had given his whole life to the kingdom. His duty was, and always had been, to King Frederick, his son and the land they fought to protect. The only person he had ever come to care about besides his family was Kit. And while the Captain respected the king greatly, he wanted to see his friend happy.

He raised his sword, and they resumed their fight. "Well, there is always a way," the Captain finally said, swishing his weapon through the air. "You are a wily young fellow, after all."

In response, Kit mimicked the Captain's move, throwing him off balance. Then he turned and dodged. Over his shoulder he asked, "And the king's wishes?"

"He's a good man, and a good king," the Captain replied thoughtfully. "If he knows that you will rule the people fairly, and keep the kingdom strong and the people happy, he will approve. I know it."

Kit smiled. "Then I pray you are wiser than you look."

Chapter Seven

*T*he day of the ball arrived quickly. As the afternoon sun began to sink, Ella found herself running back and forth between her stepsisters' and stepmother's rooms, helping the ladies prepare for the evening. Bows of various colours were thrown about. Curlers sat on the dressing table and a large selection of shoes were on display waiting to be chosen.

Standing in their bright and shiny new gowns, Anastasia and Drisella pretended to admire each other. The sisters' dresses matched in every way besides colour. Anastasia's was a bright pink, Drisella's a loud blue. Both had elaborate corsets that Ella had been forced to tie as tightly as possible.

"A vision, Sister," Anastasia said, her breathing laboured. "Truly."

Drisella nodded. "Likewise."

"We must compete for the prince's hand," Anastasia went on, picking up a fan that matched her dress. "Let it not mean we harbour dark thoughts against each other."

"Of course, dear sister," Drisella replied. "I would not dream of poisoning you before we leave for the ball."

"Or I of pushing you from the moving carriage on the way there," Anastasia countered.

As they continued slinging thinly veiled barbs at each other, Ella moved about the room, picking up discarded accessories and putting them away. She was eager to be done so that she, too, could get ready. Yet all the talk of the prince had made Ella curious.

"What will he be like, I wonder?" Ella asked.

"Like?" Anastasia laughed. "What does it matter what he's like? He's rich beyond reason!"

"Would you not like to know a bit about him before you marry him?" Ella asked, thinking of Kit and the way his dark brown hair had waved gently about his face. The way he had smiled and the way he had stuttered when she flustered him. She wanted to know more. She wanted to know everything about him.

Her sisters, it seemed, were not of the same opinion. "Certainly not!" Drisella cried. "It might change my mind."

"I bet you've never even spoken to a man," Anastasia sneered.

"I have," Ella said, Kit's face flashing in front of her again. "Once. To a gentleman."

"Some menial, no doubt," Anastasia countered. "Some 'prentice?"

Ella was unashamed. "He was an apprentice, that is true."

"All men are fools," Drisella said, parroting something her mother had said once. "The sooner you learn that, the better."

Ella did not bother to reply. Instead, she simply went back to cleaning. Not for the first time, Ella felt pity for her stepsisters. No matter how shiny or bright their dresses were, it would be difficult for them to ever know happiness with such ugly outlooks on life.

(A remarkable child, truly wise beyond her years. But I suppose I'm interrupting again. Go on, gentle reader, go on.)

A short while later, Lady Tremaine made her appearance at the top of the stairs. Unlike her daughters, whose bright dresses seemed garish and tacky, Lady Tremaine was the picture of refined elegance. Her emerald-green gown complemented her red hair, which was stylishly coiffed.

She gracefully descended the staircase and came to a stop in front of her daughters. Looking them up and down, she appraised them with a critical eye. "My dear girls," she said, "to see you like this ... it makes me believe that one of you may just snare the prince. And to think I have two horses in the race...." She kissed each of them on the cheek, then added, "I daresay no one in the kingdom will outshine my daughters."

Then, from the landing at the top of the

stairs, there came a rustle. As Lady Tremaine turned, her eyes grew narrow and her face flushed. Standing there, in a gown that was old-fashioned but infinitely more elegant than her daughters' new gowns, was Ella. Her face glowed with excitement, her eyes sparkling and her hair falling about her shoulders in perfect waves. She was, in a word, stunning.

Smiling nervously, Ella walked down the stairs. "It cost you nothing," she explained. "It's my mother's old dress, you see. And I took it up myself." She lifted the skirt of the dress to prove her point. She had spent every evening after her chores were done labouring over the dress. It had been painstaking work, but when she had finally seen herself in the small mirror in her room, she had known it was worth it. She had only wished at that moment that her mother could have been there.

Lady Tremaine took a deep breath and collected herself. The girl was far too beautiful. She needed to make sure Ella did not attend the ball under any circumstances, or Ella would undoubtedly outshine her daughters.

After living with Ella for some time, she was not so foolish as to think anger would get through to the girl. No, she needed to manipulate Ella. Bringing a hand to her heart, Lady Tremaine said, "After all I've done – feeding you, clothing you, resisting every impulse to turn you out of doors, you try to ... to embarrass me in front of the court?"

Ella was taken aback. "I ... I ... I don't want to embarrass you," she stammered. "I'm not going in order to meet the prince –"

Lady Tremaine cut her off. "There's no question of you going ... at all."

"But all of the maidens in the land are invited," Ella protested feebly. "By order of the king."

"It is the king I am thinking of," Lady Tremaine shot back. "It would be an insult to the royal personage to take you to the palace in those old rags."

"Rags," Ella repeated, the word sticking in her throat. She looked down at her mother's dress. It was one of the few reminders left of the woman who had filled this house with so much love. Bitter tears welled up in Ella's eyes and she rubbed them away. She didn't want them to see her cry. She needed to stay strong, in honour of the promises she'd made and the dress she wore.

Lady Tremaine seemed unbothered by the emotions racing across Ella's face. "This ... *thing* ..." she sneered, "is so out of style that it's practically falling to pieces. Look, the shoulder is frayed." Reaching out, Lady Tremaine pulled on the sleeve, hard. There was a loud rip and Ella gasped. But her stepmother wasn't done. She grabbed the shawl Ella had wrapped around her shoulders. Then she ripped that, too. Taking the cue from their mother, Anastasia and Drisella began to pull and tug at Ella as well. When they were done, the dress was destroyed.

Ella wrapped her arms round herself, shame and anger coursing through her body. "How could you?" she asked, her voice trembling.

"How could I otherwise?" Lady Tremaine retorted. "I will not have anyone associate my daughters with you. It would ruin their

Young Ella and her mother
save a baby bird.

Ella's father returns from a long voyage.

Ella and her family share a tearful embrace
when her mother becomes gravely ill.

Ella meets her new stepsisters,
Anastasia and Drisella.

Ella puts out some food for the mice.

With both parents gone, Ella must work as
a servant for her stepmother and stepsisters.

Ella meets a handsome apprentice in the forest.

Kit poses for his royal portrait.

Lady Tremaine forbids Ella from
attending the royal ball.

Ella's fairy godmother appears.

Ella and Kit dance with one another.

It is the perfect night.

The clock strikes midnight!

The Captain tries the glass slipper
on every maiden in the kingdom.

Kit finds Ella and returns her lost slipper to her.

Ella and Kit are wed.

prospects to be seen arriving next to a ragged servant girl." She paused, leaning in close to Ella. "Mark my words. You shall *not* go to the ball."

Later, as her stepfamily's carriage faded from view, tears filled Ella's eyes and she sank to the ground. She would never see Kit again. And she knew that after that day, her stepmother's hold on her would only tighten. Ella shuddered. Her fate seemed locked. And for once, she couldn't find the courage to smile through her pain.

Hearing footsteps behind her, Ella quickly wiped away her tears and turned. An old beggar woman stood there, leaning heavily on a gnarled wooden cane. The woman's clothes were rags and she looked ravenous. Ella felt a pang of guilt. This woman knew true hardship.

(The beggar woman! Did I not tell you she would be important? Keep going, my little reader. It's about to get very interesting.)

"Can you help me, miss?" the beggar woman asked, her voice weak. "Just a little crust of bread. Or better, a cup of milk?"

"Yes, I think I can find something for you," Ella said, pushing herself to her feet. But the action made her mother's dress, already in shreds, rip further, and the tears she had been fighting to stop started again. Focusing on the task at hand, she rushed into the house and poured a large serving of milk into a bowl. Then she carried it out to the beggar woman.

"You've been crying, my dear," the old woman said when Ella returned.

"It's nothing," Ella replied, trying to sound stronger than she felt.

The old woman shook her head. "Nothing? What is a bowl of milk? Nothing. And everything. Kindness is so rare these days," she said, taking the bowl. She sipped the milk and smiled in satisfaction. "Thank you. Now, I don't mean to hurry you, but we haven't got long, Ella." The beggar woman began to walk round to the back of the house.

Behind her, Ella cocked her head. How had the beggar woman known her name? She ran to catch up, following the woman into a large garden. "Who are you?" she asked breathlessly.

"Who am I?" the beggar woman repeated. "Well, I should think you'd have worked that out." When Ella said nothing, the woman shrugged good-naturedly. "I'm your fairy godmother, of course." (*Surprise!*)

Chapter Eight

*E*lla *nearly laughed out loud.* Her fairy godmother? "But you can't be."

The beggar woman looked genuinely surprised. "Why not?"

"Because they don't exist," Ella replied. "They're just made up. For children."

"Now, you know that's not true," the woman replied. "Didn't your own mother tell you she believed in them? And don't say no, because I heard her."

"You heard her?" Ella repeated.

Ignoring the young girl's disbelief, Ella's fairy godmother, for that was truly who she was *(it must be clear to you now, my loyal reader)*, began to look around the garden. "We really ought to get started if you're to make it to the palace in time."

"In time for what?" Ella asked.

"The ball, child. The prince's ball."

Ella sighed. Fairy godmother or not, there was no way she could go to the ball. "Look at this dress," she said, holding up the frayed ends of the pink gown. "It'll take me days to mend it, and it won't be marvellous then. And how would I get there? Even if I had something to wear? The coach has left and —"

The woman cut her off. "Oh, fiddle-faddle!" Then she paused. "First things first. Let me slip into something more comfortable."

As Ella watched, the beggar woman lifted her walking stick into the air. It suddenly transformed from an old, gnarled piece of wood into a thin silver wand. Then she began to wave the wand, causing a coil of silver glitter to descend over her head. When the glitter cleared, the beggar woman was gone, and in her place was a beautiful woman with light hair that hung about her face in tight curls.

The tattered cloak she had worn had been replaced with a white gown that sparkled.

(*Truly a spectacular transformation, if I do say so myself! I can't even begin to tell you how itchy those beggar clothes can be. I've never been fond of hessian.*)

"That's better," the Fairy Godmother said when the transformation was complete. "Now, where was I?"

Ella didn't know how it was possible or why the woman had chosen this night to appear, but she couldn't deny it any longer: the woman was most definitely magical.

"Perhaps we should begin with the carriage," the Fairy Godmother was saying. "To be honest, I hadn't really thought about it, although I can't imagine why not. Let's see...." Spinning round, she looked over the garden. In the centre, the fountain gurgled, while a greenhouse stood nearby, the strong smell of earth and flowers coming from inside. "What we need is something that sort of says 'coach'."

As her fairy godmother began to wander about, Ella followed. "That tub?" she suggested, pointing to an old claw-footed tub that was now used as a bird feeder. Her fairy godmother shook her head. "That barrel?" Again, her fairy godmother shook her head.

"I'm thinking fruits and vegetables," the woman said. "Do you grow watermelons?"

This time it was Ella's turn to shake her head.

"Cantaloupes?"

Again, Ella shook her head.

"Let me see," her fairy godmother said, racking her brain. "What about a pumpkin?" she finally suggested.

Ella's eyes lit up. "We do have pumpkins!" she said excitedly. "Here." Quickly she led her fairy godmother into the greenhouse. Inside, a whole row of pumpkins grew.

Clapping her hands in delight, Ella's fairy godmother began to inspect the pumpkins one by one. Several were far too small, others not quite ripe. Finally, she found one that seemed perfect. She tried to pick it up. But it was a rather large pumpkin and it didn't budge. "Never mind. We'll do it here."

"Do what here?" Ella asked.

"Isn't it obvious?" her fairy godmother asked, wiping dirt off her hands. "Turn the pumpkin into a carriage!"

"Oh," Ella replied, as though this were something that happened to her all the time. She looked at the pumpkin and waited for the magical transformation. And then she waited some more. Finally, she sneaked a glance at her fairy godmother. The woman's eyes were closed in concentration. Feeling Ella's gaze upon her, she opened one eye.

"Don't hurry me," she said. "I just wish I'd remembered you'd have to get there...."

(Side note: I should have brought a cantaloupe. They really are much easier to transform. Pumpkins can be so stubborn.)

"Shall I turn round?"

"It might be better..." her fairy godmother began. But then she shook her head. "Oh, for heaven's sake. Let's just have a go." Pointing her wand at the pumpkin, she mumbled a few words and a cloud of stardust blew out over the pumpkin. Then, as Ella watched in amazement, the pumpkin began to grow.

And it continued to grow.

And it grew even more.

It kept on growing until its sides pressed against the greenhouse's glass walls so hard that they shattered, sending glass and wood flying.

"Is that what you meant to do?" Ella asked.

"Do you think it's what I meant to do?"

Ella struggled to find something positive to say. After all, she didn't want to hurt her fairy godmother's feelings. "Well, it's much bigger. Well done."

"No need to patronize me, my dear," her fairy godmother retorted. Then, as if to prove her mettle, she waved her wand in the air once more.

Ella let out a gasp as, in front of her eyes, the pumpkin once again began to transform. This time, it became the most beautiful carriage she had ever seen. Fragments of the broken greenhouse became its windows, the sides grew ornate decorations and on top of the carriage, the pumpkin's stem became an immaculate roof.

Satisfied, Ella's fairy godmother began looking around the garden. "Now where are those mice?" she said. Spotting Jacqueline, Gus and their children hiding under a nearby bush, she smiled kindly. "What do you think?" she asked them. "Will you help her?"

The mice poked their noses out from under the bush. Their whiskers wiggled up and down.

The Fairy Godmother was pleased. "They said yes," she said.

"They can talk?" Ella asked, the night growing stranger still. True, her mother had told her animals could talk and listen. And true, she had spent many a lonely night telling the mice of her dreams and hardships, but she hadn't really thought they could understand her.

"Oh, certainly," her fairy godmother replied. "And they are very good listeners, too. They have told me all about you." Then, focusing her attention, she lifted her wand. In one smooth motion, she passed it over the family of mice.

As Ella watched in awe, the mice began to transform. Their faces and legs grew longer. Their haunches became more muscular and their thin tails were replaced by long hair.

Within moments, the mice were gone, and in their place stood four beautiful horses. Jacqueline had turned a fine white and grey, while Gus was midnight black. Their children, Jacob and Esau, were a stunning combination of the two.

The majestic creatures walked to the carriage and took their places in front. On her way, Jacqueline stopped and affectionately lowered her head towards Ella. Smiling, Ella patted the mare's silky mane.

With the horses and carriage taken care of, it was time to find the coachman and the footmen who would care for the horses while Ella was inside the palace. Once more her fairy godmother turned to the garden for inspiration. Two lizards became the footmen, and a goose became the coachman. When that was finished, the Fairy Godmother clapped her hands together. "Now, everyone into place. There's no time to be lost." As the coachman clambered up to his seat and one of the footmen opened the carriage door, Ella hung back. "What now, my dear?" the Fairy Godmother said. "I don't want to hurry you, but...."

Ella wrung her hands nervously. Her fairy godmother had already done so much. But.... "My dress," she finally said. "I can't go in this dress."

"What's wrong with it?" her fairy godmother asked, tilting her head and looking over the gown.

"Well, it's in pieces," Ella replied, lifting a tattered shoulder.

"Yes, yes," her fairy godmother said, nodding. "It can be very hard to tell. You see so many fashions when you're a thousand years old."

"Do you think you can mend it?" Ella asked, hope in her voice.

"I'll turn it into something new."

Ella began to shake her head vehemently. "No, no!" she cried. "This was my mother's, and I'd like to wear it when I go to the palace. It's almost, well, it's almost like taking her with me."

Her fairy godmother thought about it for

a moment. "Very well. But even your late mother won't mind if we gee it up a bit."

Before Ella could say a word, her fairy godmother waved her magic wand. Stardust surrounded Ella, and for a moment, she couldn't see through the mist. When it finally cleared, Ella stood in the most beautiful dress in the history of dresses. *(Oh, my dear, it really was. And I'm not just saying it because I made it!)*

True to her word, Ella's fairy godmother had kept elements of her mother's dress but enhanced it. The colour had changed from soft pink to sky blue. The skirt filled out and now swirled around her as she moved, and the sleeves fell slightly off her shoulders, decorated with delicate butterflies. With another wave of the wand, fireflies descended and settled into Ella's hair, around her neck and on her ears. Where they had landed, they transformed into dazzling diamonds that sparkled as they caught the moonlight. Ella was stunning.

"It is at the palace, after all," the Fairy Godmother said when she saw the astonished look on her goddaughter's face. "We might as well do things properly if we're going to do them at all. Now, off you go."

Shooting a grateful smile at her fairy godmother, Ella lifted the hem of her dress and headed towards the carriage.

"Just a moment," her fairy godmother called out, halting Ella mid-step. "Are those the best you have?"

Following her godmother's gaze, she saw that the woman was looking at her shoes. They were, Ella had to admit, a bit worn. But they were all she had, and her dress would cover them all evening, anyway. There was no need for new ones.

Her fairy godmother disagreed. "You really never do know when a little thing like shoes will matter a great deal," she said. She raised her wand, pursing her lips. "Let's have something new for a change. Then you can keep them as a memento."

As Ella took off her old shoes and placed them by the back door, her fairy godmother waved her wand one last time. There was a sparkle of magic, and then sitting there on the green lawn was a pair of beautiful glass slippers. Ella let out a gasp.

"You'll be surprised how comfortable they are," her fairy godmother commented.

(In all the years before and all the years since, I have never crafted anything quite as special as those shoes. Given the important role they played later, I'm rather glad I did. But I am getting ahead of myself. You will see just how important they were very soon.)

Gingerly, Ella slipped first one foot, then the other into her new shoes. They fit like gloves.

Her fairy godmother nodded. "Now, I really must insist you go and quickly...." Her voice trailed off as she saw a look of worry cross over Ella's face. "What is it now?"

"My stepmother and the girls," she said softly. "Won't they humiliate me and have me thrown out if they can?" Up until that moment, she had been too caught up in the magic of it all to think about it. But she knew her stepfamily all too well. They would never stand her presence at the ball.

Her fairy godmother smiled. "I can't

think why," she said. "You're invited as much as they are. But never fear. Remember, there's none so blind as those who will not see."

Ella cocked her head. "You mean they won't believe it's me, dressed as I am?"

"I *mean* I will make sure they don't know you, which I think I can do."

Ella nodded, reassured. As she took a seat on the comfortable bench inside the carriage, her fairy godmother peered through the window. "Ella, remember this: the magic will only last so long. With the echo of the last bell at the last stroke of midnight, the spell will be broken – and all will be as it was before."

"Midnight?" Ella smiled. Just moments earlier, she'd thought she wouldn't be going to the ball at all. "That will be more than enough time!"

Without further ado, the coachman gave the signal and they were off. Ella took a deep breath and leaned back. The carriage was the most elegant one she had ever been in, every inch designed to sparkle and enchant.

As the horses' hooves clopped on the road,

Ella looked out at the passing countryside. A full moon hung high in the sky, its light illuminating the roofs of houses and turning the green grasses silver. At that moment, Ella felt as if she were someone else. Someone who had never known sadness and loss. Someone who had always loved and been loved in return. At that moment, she felt like anything was possible.

Chapter Nine

I nside the palace, the ballroom glittered and shined. Several large chandeliers were lit with a thousand candles, and uniformed servers made their way through the elegantly dressed crowds offering delicious appetizers. A band was set up in the far corner of the cavernous room, the conductor's face serious as he led the musicians through their practised pieces.

Standing a bit apart from the rest of the crowd was the prince, stuck between his father and the Grand Duke. He watched as princess after princess was announced and led into the ballroom. But he barely spared them more than a first glance. Each one looked much like the others, their dresses bright and elaborate, their faces painted. None of them was the girl from the woods.

"Why do you keep looking at the stairs?" his father asked. "Who are you waiting for?"

"No one," Kit replied, not taking his gaze off the entrance.

King Frederick frowned. He was no fool. "It's that girl from the forest, isn't it?" he said. "That's why you were so generous with the invitations."

"Father!" Kit replied as though shocked. "It was for the people."

The king couldn't help smiling. At moments like this, Kit reminded him very much of the man he used to be, before the kingdom's responsibilities had weighed him down. "I know you love the people, Kit," he said kindly. "But I also know that your head has been turned." His tone grew serious. "Listen to me, my boy. You've only met her once, in the forest."

As if on cue, the Grand Duke turned to Kit,

a princess and her escort behind him. "Your Highness," he said. "May I present Princess Chelina of Zaragosa."

Kit bowed deeply. But his gaze barely swept over the princess.

"You are as handsome as your picture, Your Highness," Princess Chelina said. "And your little kingdom is enchanting."

Hearing the Grand Duke clear his throat in warning, Kit turned and met Princess Chelina's gaze. "I hope you will not find our little kingdom too confining."

"It could be bigger ... with the right friends. And enough soldiers," she replied.

"I'm not sure I understand," Kit said.

Princess Chelina put a hand on Kit's arm. "Of course you do," she said. "They tell me you are very brave in battle."

Kit stifled a groan. This princess in front of him had no interest in him, just as he had no interest in her. All she wanted was the power an alliance provided. Kit certainly wanted the best for his kingdom, but he knew that this would not be won by war or strategic alliances.

It would be won with kindness, courage and love.

Suddenly, Kit noticed that while he and Princess Chelina had been talking, a hushed silence had fallen over the crowd. Everyone's attention had been caught by a commotion at the grand staircase. As Kit turned to see what was going on, his breath caught in his throat.

For standing there, at the top of the stairs, was the girl from the woods.

Gone were her simple gown and her dishevelled hair. Now she was wearing the most elegant dress Kit had ever seen. Her hair glistened and sparkled, diamonds peeking out of her long waves. While every eye in the room was on her, the girl was the picture of calm. She seemed unaware of her own beauty and the reaction she was inspiring in the crowd. It took every ounce of self-control for Kit not to run to her side. Instead, he bowed to Chelina. "Excuse me," he said, walking away.

Behind him, Kit could hear the Grand Duke making apologies on his behalf.

But Princess Chelina waved him off.

"Who is that?" she asked, pointing at the woman who had caught the prince's attention.

"I have no idea, Your Highness," the Grand Duke said. But he was determined to find out.

As Ella stood at the top of the stairs, her heart pounded in her ears. The crowd was a sea of bright colours below her, everyone's face a blur. Except for his. Except for Kit's. She saw him almost immediately. He stood at the opposite end of the room, dressed in a cream-coloured suit that made his shoulders seem broader and his face even more handsome. As if pulled by an invisible string, Ella made her way down the stairs. At the same time, she saw Kit manoeuvre his way through the crowd.

Finally, after what felt like the longest walk of her life, Ella found herself face-to-face with Kit. They stood at the edge of the dance floor, both momentarily at a loss for words. Kit seemed oddly nervous, almost tongue-tied at the sight of her. Despite the butterflies in her stomach, Ella smiled and said a silent thank-you again to her fairy godmother.

"Mr Kit ..." Ella finally said.

Kit shook his head as if coming out of a dream. "It's you ... isn't it?" he asked.

Ella nodded shyly. "Just so."

"If I may – That is –" Kit stammered. "It would give me the greatest pleasure if you would, uh, that is, if you would do me the honour of letting me lead you through the – the next...." His voice trailed off, as though he were searching for the right word.

"Dance?" Ella guessed.

Kit nodded, relieved. "Yes, dance. That's it."

A wave of excitement washed over Ella. Nodding, she gave him a shy smile, and he held out his hand. She took it, and he drew her onto the dance floor. As he did so, the guests all around them bowed.

"They are all looking at you," Ella said, a bit confused.

But Kit shook his head. "Believe me, they are all looking at you."

Then, before she could say another word, Kit placed his free hand gently on Ella's hip. She took a sharp breath and met Kit's gaze.

He was staring down at her, his eyes full of wonder. As the music began, they moved together. Soon other couples joined them on the dance floor. But Ella took no notice. She only had eyes for Kit. And while there were many things she wanted to say, Ella knew that she should just take in this perfect moment. So she let herself go, her steps in time with Kit's, his hand warm in hers.

As Ella danced with her boy from the woods, she was unaware that her appearance was causing quite the fuss among certain guests. At the edge of the dance floor, Lady Tremaine stared at the girl, trying to figure out why she seemed so familiar. Beside her, Anastasia and Drisella were marvelling at the girl's gorgeous gown and were surprised when their mother snapped at them. "You must turn the prince's head, you fools!" she hissed. "Get out there!"

"But no one has asked us to dance," Anastasia said.

Lady Tremaine sighed deeply. Seeing two gentlemen about to walk past, she shoved her daughters in front of them. The startled men bowed. Then, before they could protest, they found themselves being pushed onto the dance floor by Lady Tremaine. As she watched her daughters clumsily manoeuvre their way closer to the prince, she stifled a groan. Both girls batted their eyelashes and tried to smile alluringly. But the prince didn't even notice. He could not take his eyes off the girl in his arms.

The crowd slowly exited the dance floor, leaving the prince and his partner alone. They made a beautiful pair as they swept over the floor, their steps in perfect sync. When the music came to a stop, there was a moment of silence, and then the crowd burst into applause, sure they had just witnessed the prince and his future princess in their first dance. The Grand Duke watched as Kit leaned down and whispered something into the girl's ear. She nodded, and then the two of them walked off the floor, disappearing through one of the big ballroom doors.

Who is that girl? The Grand Duke started to panic in his spot on the balcony. Luckily, at that moment the Captain of the Guard returned. The Grand Duke had sent him to find out anything he could about the mystery woman.

"People are saying she is a princess," the Captain reported. "Our prince seems quite taken with her. You do not approve?" he asked when he noticed the sour look on the other man's face.

"He is already promised to the princess Chelina of Zaragosa!" the Grand Duke shouted manically.

Suddenly, a small noise came from behind them. The two men turned and found themselves looking at Lady Tremaine. She curtsied with a flourish.

"I didn't mean to intrude," she said, bringing her green fan to her face and moving to leave.

Then she suddenly spoke again. "Your secret is safe with me," she added before hastily exiting the balcony.

The Grand Duke glared after her, wondering what to do about the mystery princess.

Chapter Ten

Meanwhile, unaware that anyone was looking for them, Kit and Ella walked down the long castle gallery. The walls were lined with portraits of previous rulers and their families, their faces looking down upon the pair.

Ella's mind was reeling. As they had finished the most perfect dance, she was unable to miss the way the crowd had bowed low as they had passed. It had seemed odd to her, until she realized that as they bowed, they also said, "Your Highness." She had looked at Kit in bewilderment. It was then that he had leaned down and asked her to join him in the gallery.

Now Ella was trying to make sense of it all. She had thought she was dancing with just a boy ... an apprentice of some sort. But this was obviously no regular boy. Had he been playing her for a fool all along? He had seemed real and honest. Now she didn't know. The promise she had made to her mother echoed through her head. *Have courage.* She took a deep breath. She would find out the truth.

"So you are the prince," Ella said.

"Well, not *the* prince exactly. There are plenty of princes in the world. I'm only *a* prince," Kit said, trying to lighten the moment.

"I see," she replied. "But you are not an apprentice."

"I am," Kit said quickly. "An apprentice monarch. Still learning the trade." When Ella didn't say anything, Kit scrambled to find the words. "Please forgive me. I thought you might treat me differently if you knew. I mistook *you* for a simple country girl. But now I see that you didn't want to overawe a plain soldier."

Ella looked down, thinking it through. This was Kit, even if he was really a prince.

"So," Kit said, holding out his hand, "no more surprises?"

Ella paused and then took his hand. "No more surprises," she repeated.

A relieved smile spread across Kit's face, and Ella found herself once again captivated by his handsome features. Nervously, Ella looked away, her gaze landing on the portrait in front of them. It was a sizable painting of Kit riding a majestic horse. He was larger than life, his hand holding a sword high in the air, his eyes trained on something in the distance. She was surprised she hadn't noticed before: he was every bit a prince.

"Is that you?" Ella asked.

Kit nodded. "I hate myself in paintings," he said sheepishly. "Don't you?"

Ella let out a nervous laugh. "No one has ever painted my portrait."

"Well they should," Kit said.

Ella felt her face flush. She looked back up at the wall. "What were you doing?"

"That?" Kit said, pointing at the picture. "Oh, I was about to charge the enemy."

"How terrible!" Ella replied.

Kit raised an eyebrow. "Most people would say, 'How exciting!'"

"I'm sorry."

"Don't be," the prince said. "You're right. It is terrible. I'm not supposed to say that ... but it is."

Before Ella could ask him more questions, Kit took her hand in his. As she looked down at their interlaced fingers, all other thoughts left her mind. She followed as Kit led her out of the gallery and into the gardens behind the palace.

The full moon bathed everything in a silver glow. A large ornamental fountain stood in the middle of the grounds. Water sprayed out of the mouths of ceramic fish, and several Greek gods stood captured forever in stone. Cupid and his bow seemed to be aimed right at Ella and Kit as they walked past.

Kit smiled. "Here is where I played when I was little," he said.

"With whom did you play?" Ella asked, imagining a young Kit, with dishevelled dark waves and covered with grass.

"The Captain of the Guard, kind fellow that he was," Kit replied. "Who did you have to play with?"

"Oh, I had so many playmates!" Ella answered, a big smile spreading across her face. "Sheep and geese, and all the mice, of course."

Kit looked at Ella, trying to see if she was teasing him. Then she added, "They are excellent listeners."

Kit smiled. This girl continued to amaze him. She was so wise, yet so innocent. So sweet, yet he could tell she was strong. He felt as though he'd only scratched the surface, and he longed to find out more about her. Kit had to admit the ball had turned out to be quite the good idea after all.

They continued to walk around the grounds, past rosebushes, a grove of trees with ivory petals blooming on the branches, and various other well manicured plants and flowers. Passing a particularly lovely ornamental urn, Ella clapped her hands. "How beautiful!" she exclaimed.

A sad smile tugged at the corner of Kit's mouth. "My mother loved it here," he said softly. "Since she died, my father can't bring himself to visit the gardens."

Ella squeezed his hand. "My mother is in heaven, too," she said. "Do you suppose they know each other?"

Kit was touched by Ella's sweetness. "I don't see why not."

"I think heaven is like this ball," Ella declared. "Everyone is invited."

"That's because of you," Kit replied. When Ella looked at him in confusion, he went on. "I made sure that everyone could come because ... well, because I hoped to see you again."

Ella looked up at him. He had planned all this for her? It was overwhelming. "And I came," she finally said, "to see Mr Kit."

"Not the prince?" Kit asked, teasing her.

"Oh, no," Ella replied playfully. "The prince is far too grand."

"Surely not for someone like you," Kit said. "I don't suppose you have a large army?"

Ella shook her head. "I'm afraid I have no army at all."

Kit shrugged. He hadn't expected her to say yes, though it would have made things a great deal easier.

"Won't they miss you at the ball?" Ella asked.

"Maybe," he said. "But let's not go back just yet."

Ella looked worried. "What's wrong?"

"When I go back, they will try to pair me off with a lady of their choosing," Kit replied, his honesty surprising Ella. "I am expected to marry for advantage."

"Surely you've a right to your own heart," Ella said, shocked by this notion.

Kit shook his head. "I must weigh that against the king's wishes. He is a wise ruler, and a loving father."

"Perhaps he will change his mind," Ella suggested.

Once again, Kit shook his head. "I fear he hasn't much time to do so."

Ella felt a pang of sympathy. She reached out

a hand and gently touched his arm. Poor Kit. He was a good person, a sweet and thoughtful man who listened to what people had to say. He did not deserve so much pain.

"Would you like to see my very favourite place?" Kit's question caught Ella off guard. She had been so lost in thoughts of what the future held she'd forgotten to enjoy the moment while she could. She nodded.

Kit led her away from the more formal gardens. As they headed farther down the path, nature seemed to take over. The bushes grew wilder, the trees' leaves hung lower and the grass grew higher. It was a romantic garden, full of life and wild beauty.

"A secret garden!" Ella said with delight.

"I've never shown this to anyone," Kit said, pulling aside a few branches to reveal an old wooden swing. He offered the seat to Ella.

"I shouldn't," she protested.

But Kit wouldn't listen. "You should."

Ella gingerly took a seat, the wood creaking beneath her. Kit moved behind her and placed both hands on the small of her back, his touch hesitant. "May I?" he asked, his voice a whisper in her ear.

Ella's heart fluttered and she felt goosebumps on her arms. "Please," she said breathlessly.

Ever so gently, Kit pushed Ella forward. She tucked her knees under the seat, sending the swing back to him. As the swing squeaked, Ella laughed. She hadn't been on a swing in years, and she felt foolish and alive. It reminded her of riding Galahad in the forest, the cool wind rushing past her.

Kit gave her an even harder push and Ella flew high into the air. As the seat reached its peak, one of her shoes flew off and landed in the grass a short distance away. Ella let out a surprised, "Oh!"

Kit raced to retrieve the shoe as Ella slowed the swing until she was still. "It's made of glass," Kit said in a tone of wonder. He was holding the shoe very carefully in his hand.

"And why not?" Ella replied with a twinkle in her eye.

Kneeling down in front of Ella, Kit gently slid the slipper back onto her foot. Their eyes met. The garden suddenly seemed hushed. Ella felt herself holding her breath, lost in the beauty of the moment.

"There," Kit finally said, his voice full of unspoken emotion. He stood up.

"There," Ella said, her voice equally soft. Then she, too, stood up.

Face-to-face, they lingered. The moment was pure and simple. Beautiful and romantic. It was perfect. And then Kit spoke again and Ella realized it was not altogether real.

"Won't you tell me who you really are?" he asked.

"If I do," Ella began, struggling to find the right words, "I think everything might be ... different."

"I don't understand," Kit said. "Can you at least tell me your name?"

Ella couldn't seem to catch her breath. She felt as though her ribs were tightening round her heart. This was it. He had been nothing but honest with her that evening, and he was only asking her name. Once again her mother's words echoed in her head. *Have courage. Be kind.*

Now was the time. "My name is ..." she began. "My name is...."

Ella's eyes grew wide as she looked up at the large clock atop one of the palace's towers. It was nearly 12 o'clock. "I have to leave!" she cried. Kit looked at her, confused. "It's hard to explain. Lizards, pumpkins...." She didn't bother to go on. Instead, with one last look at Kit, she turned and ran.

Chapter Eleven

*E*lla ran as fast as her glass slippers would allow. She heard Kit call out to her to wait. Turning to see his bewildered expression, she knew she had to say something.

"You've been awfully nice," Ella called. "Thank you for a wonderful evening. I loved it. Every second." Then she ran through the garden, to the terrace, and up the stone steps. She found herself standing in front of the door to the gallery where their walk had begun. Moving through the doors, she disappeared into the darkness of the gallery.

She raced past the portraits and burst into the ballroom a moment later. Ducking and weaving among the dancers, she safely made her way across the room, but then – *smack!* – she ran right into King Frederick.

"Oh!" Ella exclaimed. "Your Highness!"

He nodded at the pretty girl in front of him. "Young lady."

"I'm ... I'm so sorry!" Ella said, starting to rush away. But once again, she got the feeling that she couldn't leave it there. She turned back. "I wanted to say, Your Highness, that your son, Kit, is the most lovely person I ever met. So good and brave. I hope you know how much he loves you." Without another word, she raced off, leaving the king with a bemused expression on his face.

Ella ran faster than she had ever run before. She ran up the ballroom steps and down the long hall. She ran past guests who'd stepped outside for a breath of fresh air. She dodged a small dog eating scraps but couldn't avoid knocking over a tray of sweets as she passed a servant. She wanted to stop to help, but she knew she couldn't. Not if she wanted to get back to the carriage in time.

Finally, she found herself at the top of the staircase leading down to the palace courtyard. She spotted her carriage nearby. With a sigh of relief, she ran down the stairs. Suddenly, she felt one of her glass slippers, the one that had flown off on the swing, slide off her foot once more. She was just about to fetch it when she saw a group of guards arrive at the top of the stairs. With one last sad look at her pretty shoe, Ella ran the rest of the way down the stairs.

One of the footmen leaned against the side of the carriage, trying to catch a fly. As soon as he spotted Ella, he frantically motioned to the coachman, the fly forgotten. With a snap of the reins, the coachman started moving the carriage and Ella slipped inside. Then the carriage was off, the four noble horses racing into the night.

Letting out a deep breath, Ella finally looked back. She could just make out the prince standing on the steps. In one hand, he held her glass slipper. But it wasn't the loss of the shoe that hurt; it was the expression on his face that broke Ella's heart. Kit looked confused and sad. And it was all her fault.

As the carriage sped out the palace gates, Ella heard the bells tolling the midnight hour. She also heard the sound of hoofbeats and knew that the guards were in pursuit. That meant Kit didn't want her to go. But she couldn't let him find her. Not now, not when the magic was about to end. Ella saw that her kind lizard footman had closed the gates behind them. As the guards reached them, they had to pull them open once more, giving Ella's carriage the chance to travel farther ahead.

The bell tolled again. Ella leaned out the window and saw the horses' tails begin to transform back into mouse tails. Around her, the walls of the carriage started to turn orange. As the persistent bell tolled loudly, the coachman's nose grew back into a beak, and he let out an anxious honk.

A short distance behind, unaware of any of these odd changes, the guards continued their pursuit. Among them were the Grand Duke and the Captain. They both wanted to catch the mystery princess but for different reasons. The Grand Duke wanted to expose her for the fake he thought she was, while the Captain simply wanted to make Kit happy.

Inside the carriage, Ella listened to each toll of the bell with a growing sense of dread. They were running out of time and needed to get away from the guards before it was too late.

The horses' ears became round, and their muzzles narrowed into snouts. Then the coachman transformed completely back into a goose, his uniform falling around his webbed feet. The carriage itself began to shake and the footmen became lizards once more.

As a cloud passed over the moon, Ella's carriage clattered over a bridge, bringing them farther from their pursuers and closer to home. But they still had a long way to go, and as the ninth bell tolled, the carriage began to resemble a pumpkin, its elegant symmetry replaced with a bulbous shape and a wooden stub protruding from the top. At the tenth bell, the horses finally disappeared, replaced by the four mice, who let out frightened squeaks as the pumpkin carriage rolled on. The goose fell to the road, honking loudly before shaking himself off and flying the rest of the way home. And as the eleventh and twelfth bells tolled, the spell was broken.

With the sounds of the last bell fading away, Ella found herself sitting on the ground, the pumpkin cracked beside her. There was a slight whoosh as her jewels transformed back into fireflies, and then, last but not least, her beautiful gown became the torn and ragged dress from before. All that was left of the magic was a single glass slipper. Ella pushed herself to her feet and began to brush herself off. Then she heard hoofbeats. She looked up ... right into the cold, calculating eyes of the Grand Duke.

"Identify yourself," the Duke said.

For a moment, Ella was taken aback. He didn't recognize her. But then again, why would he? All he probably saw was a grubby servant girl on the side of the road. "They call me Cinderella," she replied, happy to keep her identity a secret. It seemed her stepfamily's cruel nickname was coming in handy.

The Grand Duke dismounted. As he began to walk round her, inspecting her like cattle, she slid the remaining slipper into a fold of her dress. "Cinderella?" the man repeated. "What sort of name is that? Who are you?"

"Me?" Ella replied. "I am no one."

"You certainly don't look like anyone," the Duke replied, an expression of distaste on his face. "And yet ... that dress looks familiar. Were you at the ball?"

"Who could wear these rags to the ball, sir?" Ella asked innocently.

The Grand Duke still looked suspicious. "There was a carriage on the road. With a princess inside...." His voice trailed off but his meaning was clear enough. He wanted to know if she had seen the carriage or, better yet, if she knew the princess inside.

"I don't know any princesses, my lord," Ella answered honestly.

"No," the Duke said. "How could you? Yet ... there is something about you...."

He leaned closer and Ella took an involuntary step back, shaken by his cold eyes. Luckily, the sound of more hoofsteps interrupted the Grand Duke. Ella saw that the guards had arrived, led by their captain. Moving away from Ella, the Grand Duke shook his head. "No, you do not look like her," he said. "Only a servant girl after all. Filthy and quite rank. You smell like a rodent." Turning, he nodded to the Captain of the Guard. "Escort this girl home."

"That's not necessary," Ella said. "I know the way." Then, before anyone could protest, she disappeared into the trees alongside the road.

When she was sure she wasn't being followed, Ella let out a sigh. That had been too close for comfort. And she still had to get back to the house before her stepfamily returned. She ushered the mice into her remaining glass slipper so she could walk them the rest of the way.

A light rain began to fall. Ella cupped her

hand over the slipper so the mice would not get wet and made her way back to the house. She heard the sound of a carriage approaching. Ducking to the side of the drive, she rushed through the pantry and into the kitchen just as she heard her stepsisters clatter through the front door. There was murmuring as the girls bickered, and then, much to Ella's dismay, she heard their footsteps moving closer.

Acting quickly, she let her mice friends climb out of the glass slipper before putting the shoe into the hearth and covering it with ashes. Then she lay down beside the hearth and closed her eyes.

When Anastasia and Drisella entered the kitchen, they found their stepsister sleeping, covered in the ashes that had inspired her nickname.

"Look at that," Anastasia sneered. "She fell asleep in that *thing* she was wearing."

"She must be dreaming about going to the ball," Drisella added. "Wake her up so we can tell her all about it."

Anastasia shook her head. "What she doesn't know won't hurt her."

"I know! That's why I want to wake her." Drisella leaned down and shouted into Ella's ear. "Get up, lazybones!"

Ella opened her eyes and then stretched, as if she had been asleep for hours.

"You missed it!" Drisella crowed.

"Oh? What happened?" Ella asked.

"You can't even imagine," Anastasia said as her sister ordered Ella to prepare a plate of biscuits and warm some tea.

As Ella started to prepare the snack, her sisters began to recount the events of the night. They were interrupted by their mother, who entered and immediately demanded that their treats be brought to the parlour. She wasn't going to let them start eating in the kitchen like scullery maids ... or Cinderella. Once she and her daughters were settled, the girls continued talking. As usual, they were talking more *at* Ella than to her.

"The prince was showing me a great deal of favour," Anastasia said.

"I thought his eye was more inclined towards me," Drisella argued.

Ella couldn't help herself. "What did he say to you?" she asked, knowing full well he hadn't spoken a word.

There was a pause as the sisters looked at each other. "What do you mean, what did he say?" Anastasia finally said.

Drisella had an answer. "Don't be so common, Cinderella," she snapped. "We did not communicate with mere words. Our souls met."

Lady Tremaine, who had been silent up until that point, finally seemed to lose her patience. "You didn't speak to him, let alone dance!" she snapped.

"It was not our fault, Mother!" Anastasia whined. "It was that *girl*...."

"The mystery princess!" Drisella added.

"That was no princess," Lady Tremaine said, her eyes on Ella as she spoke. The girl seemed oddly lighthearted despite having been forced to stay home. It made Lady Tremaine suspicious. "It was a preening interloper who made a spectacle of herself. A vulgar young hussy marched into the ball and threw herself at the prince."

"And he actually danced with the ugly thing," Anastasia added.

Ella looked down, trying to hide the smile that threatened to spread across her face. Unaware that her stepmother was watching her, she hummed a few bars of the song she and Kit had danced to, lost in the memory of that perfect moment.

"Yes?" she said dreamily.

"Yes!" Drisella repeated. "It was pity. He was too polite to send her packing in front of everyone, you see. But not wanting to expose us to the presumptuous wench any further, he took her aside –"

Anastasia jumped in, interrupting her sister. "And told her off! But she refused to leave, and the palace guard had to chase her from the party."

Ella could barely contain the laughter that bubbled up inside her. It was amazing how quickly her stepsisters could make themselves believe anything as long as it benefited them.

Glancing at Lady Tremaine, she saw that the woman was watching her with narrowed eyes. Ella quickly looked back at the ground, worried she might have given herself away.

"It's no matter," Lady Tremaine finally said. "The ball was a mere diversion. The prince is promised to Princess Chelina of Zaragosa. The Grand Duke told me as much himself." Then she turned and spoke the next words right to Ella. "He's not allowed to marry for love."

Ella sat in her draughty attic room, staring at the glass slipper she held in her hand. Her mind kept replaying moments from the ball: seeing Kit for the first time; feeling his hand in hers; swinging in the wild garden. The memories flashed through her mind, each one vivid and perfect. Yet her stepmother had said the prince could not marry for love. If that was true, she and Kit could never have a future. Not that she was sure he would want a future with her, or she with him. She shook her head to clear her thoughts.

Sighing, Ella stood up and walked to the far corner of the attic. She kneeled down and lifted up a loose floorboard. Inside was the beautiful toy butterfly her father had given to her many years earlier. She gently placed the slipper next to it and then put the board back in place. Noticing that Jacqueline, Gus and their children were watching from nearby, Ella smiled. She hadn't seen them since the magical transformation.

"Thank you for your help," she said. "It really was like a dream. Better than a dream." Then she squared her shoulders. "But now it's done."

Jacqueline and Gus rose on their hind legs and attempted to imitate dancing. Ella laughed, amused by her friends' efforts. But they had made a point. The ball hadn't been a dream. It had been real. And the way she felt when she was around Kit? That was real, too.

She thought about his spirit, his courage, his kindness. She thought about the way she had felt dancing in his arms. She loved talking to him; she loved being silent with him. He was one of those rare souls who made one feel comfortable no matter what.

And now he was promised to another. It made Ella's heart hurt to think he did not have control over such an important decision. She wished she could do something to help him.

Sighing once more, Ella smoothed the front of her apron. At least they would forever have the fond memory of the perfect night at the ball.

Chapter Twelve

Kit entered his father's bedroom. His heart pounded in his ears, and his vision blurred as his eyes adjusted to the darkness of the room. The curtains had been drawn on the windows of the round chamber. The royal physician was kneeling by the king's bed, finishing his examination. Hearing Kit, the doctor stood up and moved towards the door. Kit saw the expression on the doctor's face, and he knew what it meant: the king had little time left.

When they were alone, Kit strode to his father's bedside. The older man struggled to open his eyes. Upon seeing Kit, King Frederick smiled. "You've come," he said weakly. "Good."

Kit gulped. He had known his father was ill, but he had never allowed himself to believe that their time together would be so limited. "Father," Kit started, sounding like a young boy. "What's happened?"

"What happens to us all in time, my boy," King Frederick replied.

"Not to you," Kit said, trying to boost his father's spirits, even though they both knew it was futile. "Not to my king. Not to my father. You will recover."

The king smiled. "You must learn to lie better than that if you will be a good statesman."

Overwhelmed, Kit sank down on the bed, taking his father's hand in his. The hand he held was frail, the fingers thin and trembling. This was the hand that had held him when he was little. The hand that had signed peace treaties and the hand that had carried a sword. And now.... "Father," Kit pleaded, tears welling in his eyes, "don't go."

"I must," the king said. "But you needn't be alone. Take a bride." When Kit began to shake his head, the king went on. "What if I commanded you to do so?"

That is unfair, Kit thought. But he had no desire to argue with his father on the man's deathbed. "I know that you want me to marry for advantage," Kit began.

"And ... ?" his father said.

"And I will not." The words came out in a rush. "I'm sorry. I love and respect you, but I won't. I believe we need not look outside of our borders for strength or guidance. What we need is right before us. We need only...." He paused, remembering what the mystery princess had said to him when they first met. "We need only have courage and be kind to see it."

Silence filled the chamber. King Frederick closed his eyes, and for one moment of panic, Kit worried he had said too much. Then King Frederick's eyes opened again. And to Kit's surprise, he nodded. "Just so," the king said, pride in his voice. "You have become your own man. Good. And perhaps, in the little time left to me, I can become the father you deserve."

This was not what Kit had expected. What

did his father mean, become the father he deserved? While they didn't always see eye to eye, the king had been a loving and good father.

"You must not marry for advantage," the king said. "You must marry for love. Find that girl they are all talking about. The forgetful one who loses her shoes."

Kit broke into a sad smile. "But the Grand Duke...."

"He will never rule so long as you are not mastered by him," King Frederick said, his voice growing weaker. "Be cheerful, my boy. Have courage, and be kind."

Kit smiled at the familiar words. He had been given the greatest gift – freedom. Freedom to choose and freedom to love. He didn't know what to say except, "Thank you, Father."

With great effort, King Frederick pushed himself up on the bed so he could look his son in the eye. "I love you."

As night fell beyond the curtains, father and son, king and prince, sat together in silence, happy to have this moment and aware they needed to cherish it for as long as they both could.

Chapter Thirteen

*F*or a month after King Frederick's death, black funeral bunting hung across shop fronts, and a general sadness hung over the kingdom. But after a while, the time for mourning came to an end. And when it did, a proclamation from the palace was sent out.

It happened by chance while Ella was in the market, where she had first heard news of the ball. Now she was with her stepsisters, helping them shop, which entailed carrying their bags. Ella drifted towards a commotion in the town square, her sisters following.

The royal crier was once again standing on the edge of the fountain, reading from a large scroll. "Hear ye! Hear ye!" he cried. "Know that our new king hereby declares his love for the mysterious princess who wore glass slippers to the ball, and requests she present herself at the palace, whereupon, if she be willing, he will forthwith marry her, with all due ceremony."

For Ella, it was as if time had stopped. The prince loved the mystery princess? *Kit* loved *her*? After believing that the magical night at the ball would be the last time she ever saw Kit, Ella's hope sprang anew. Kit was declaring his love for her. A blush crept up Ella's cheeks, and she felt her heart come alive.

Without a word to her stepsisters, she turned and raced back towards the house. She needed to get to the palace as soon as possible. There was no way she was going to be able to present herself in the beautiful gown she had worn to the ball, but she did have one thing that would help her prove her identity – the glass slipper. Ella laughed, thinking about what her fairy godmother had said that magical night: "You really never do know when a little thing like shoes will matter a great deal." Oh, how right she had been.

(See, loyal reader? Didn't I tell you fairy godmothers are always right?)

But when she rushed into her room and pried the floorboard loose, she let out a cry. The only thing in her hiding spot was the toy butterfly. And its wings had been ripped off.

"Are you looking for this?"

Ella whipped round. Her stepmother was sitting in a chair, her face half shadowed, her eyes gleaming. She held Ella's glass slipper.

"There must be quite a story to go with it," Lady Tremaine said, dangling the slipper off one finger. "Will you tell me?" Ella shook her head. "Then *I* will tell *you* a story. There once was a beautiful young girl, who married for love. She had two loving daughters. All was well. But then her husband, the light of her life, died. The next time, she married for the sake of her children. But this man, too, was taken from her." She smiled at Ella, but it was a cold smile that didn't reach her eyes.

"And I was doomed to look every day upon his beloved child."

Lady Tremaine stopped, and for a moment, she and Ella just stared at each other. A part of Ella, the part that had experienced the loss of loved ones, felt for her stepmother. But another part, the part that remembered Lady Tremaine's cruel treatment, felt no sympathy.

Lady Tremaine went on with her story. "I had hoped to marry off one of my beautiful, stupid daughters to the prince. But his head was turned by a girl with glass slippers. And so ... I lived unhappily ever after. And so my story would appear to be ended. Now, tell me yours." She held up the slipper. "Did you steal it?"

Ella shook her head. "It was given to me."

"Given to you? Given to *you*?" Her stepmother let out a cruel laugh. "Nothing is ever given. For everything, we must pay and pay."

"That's not true," Ella said. "Kindness is free. Love is free."

Anger flashed across Lady Tremaine's face. "You're wrong. Love costs us everything." The slipper swayed under the woman's finger and Ella watched fearfully. If it fell and broke, she would have nothing to show Kit. As if reading her thoughts, Lady Tremaine told Ella what would happen next.

She, a lady, would vouch for Ella. After all, who would believe a servant girl with no family was the beautiful 'princess' who had stolen the prince's heart? When Ella and the prince were married, Ella would make Lady Tremaine the head of the royal household and ensure that Anastasia and Drisella were married to wealthy lords. Lady Tremaine would be assured a place in society for the rest of her days, and as head of household, she informed Ella, she would control the palace.

Ella's hands shook as her stepmother outlined the plan. She had tried with every fibre of her being to put on a brave front in the face of her stepmother's cruelty. She had tended to all the housework, to every whim and desire of her stepfamily. She had lived in the attic of her own home. She had become Cinderella. She had given up so much. But she was tired of it.

She wouldn't let her stepmother take anything more. "No," she said.

"No?" Lady Tremaine repeated.

"I will not allow you to ruin the palace the way you have ruined my home," Ella said. "I was not able to protect my father from you, but I will protect Kit, and the kingdom."

Lady Tremaine's eyes narrowed and her cheeks grew red. "So you are courageous to boot. That is a mistake." Lifting her hand high in the air, she smashed the glass slipper against the wall. It shattered, leaving Lady Tremaine holding a single large shard.

Ella let out a gasp. "Why are you so cruel?" she cried. "I don't understand. I have tried to be kind, though you do not deserve it. Why do you do it? Why?"

The question seemed to unhinge Lady Tremaine. "Why?" she yelled back. "Because you are young and innocent and good, and I ... I ... I am not." Without another word she stormed out, slamming the door and locking it behind her.

Ella rushed over. But she knew it was useless

before she even got there. She was trapped. And her stepmother was free to do and say whatever she pleased.

Lady Tremaine wasted no time in doing just that. As soon as she was sure Cinderella couldn't leave the attic, she brought the shard of slipper to the one person she knew she could count on – the Grand Duke.

"May I ask where you got this?" he enquired when Lady Tremaine showed him the shard.

Lady Tremaine nodded demurely. "From a ragged servant girl in my household," she answered.

The Grand Duke looked down at the glass, his expression thoughtful.

"And you came straight to me?"

"Of course," Lady Tremaine answered. "I have heard that you are the most honourable man in the kingdom."

They exchanged smiles.

"And the girl...."

"Is in a safe place," she finished.

The man nodded. "You have spared the

kingdom from a great deal of embarrassment,"
he said.

Lady Tremaine looked pleased. This was
just what she had hoped would happen, for
now the Grand Duke owed her. When she
made that clear, he asked what she wanted. The
answer came quickly. "A title for myself," Lady
Tremaine said. "And advantageous marriages
for my two daughters."

"Done," he agreed. "And the girl?"

"Do with her what you will," Lady Tremaine
said, waving a hand in the air. "She's nothing
to me."

The Grand Duke tested the sharp point of
the shard on his finger. "Well," he said after
a moment, "the young king will take some
convincing. He is ... wilful. But keep this girl
out of sight until we may profitably marry him
off, and you will get what you desire."

Lady Tremaine smirked. She would be more
than willing to keep Cinderella out of sight –
for as long as necessary.

Kit was exhausted. Since his father's death, he had barely slept, and once he had sent out the proclamation seeking his mystery princess, sleep had been even more elusive. He stared out the window of the throne room. The Captain of the Guard stood nearby, a comforting presence. If only Kit could find the girl he couldn't stop thinking about....

Hearing footsteps, Kit looked up. The Grand Duke was striding across the room, a barely suppressed smile on his face. Coming to a stop in front of him, the Grand Duke held out a glass shard. Kit recognized it instantly.

"Where ... ?" he began.

"Abandoned on the side of the road," the Grand Duke answered.

Kit held the shard in his hand, tracing the edge with his thumb. "And have you found her?"

"No," the older man said. "She has completely disappeared."

"There must be some reason she vanished," Kit said, refusing to give up all hope.

The girl he knew from the woods was strong and courageous. She wouldn't run away. A dark thought raced through his head. "Perhaps she has been prevented from speaking...."

At the suggestion, the Grand Duke shifted uncomfortably. Kit noticed and was about to press him when the other man spoke, his words a knife to Kit's heart.

"It pains me to say this, Your Highness, but has it occurred to you that the maiden might not return your feelings?"

He paused, letting the words sink in. "She may see you as our enemies do: the callow, naive princeling of a weak little monarchy. Perhaps ... she simply does not love you."

Kit flinched as though struck. "I knew you were cynical, Grand Duke. I did not know you were cruel."

"The world is cruel, Your Highness," the Grand Duke replied. "Not I."

Until then, the Captain of the Guard had been silent. He was surprised to hear the Grand Duke speak to the young king this way, and he didn't like it. "Don't lose heart, Kit," the Captain said, trying to help.

The Grand Duke shot the Captain a look. "On the contrary," he said. "Lose heart and gain wisdom. The people need to know that the kingdom is secure. That the king has a queen. They want to face the future with certainty."

For a moment, Kit was silent, the Grand Duke's words ringing in his ears. The older man did have a point. But on his deathbed, his father had told him that the only way the Grand Duke could ever rule was for Kit to let him. And Kit was not ready to roll over and give up. Not yet.

"Now *I* am king," Kit said. "And *I* say we must seek out the mystery princess. Even if she does not want to be found. I have to see her again." His eyes narrowed and he focused his next words directly at the Grand Duke. "That is my command."

The Grand Duke nodded reluctantly. "As you will, Your Majesty. But if she is not found, then for the good of the kingdom, you must marry the princess Chelina." He knew there was no hope of finding the mystery princess. What harm would it do to let the newly crowned king think he was in control?

Kit hesitated. He did not want to marry Princess Chelina. But if agreeing meant he could continue his search for the girl from the woods, he would say what was needed. "Very well. But you will spare no effort." His fate, his heart and his kingdom were on the line.

Chapter Fourteen

*T*he search began almost *immediately.*
Led by the Grand Duke and the Captain
of the Guard, a group set off from the palace.
As ordered, they were to visit every maiden in
the kingdom, whether she was rich or poor.
Kit had placed the glass slipper in the Grand
Duke's keeping to be used as a test. If the shoe
fitted, they had found their mystery princess.

And so it began. They knocked on the
doors of large homes where the ladies greeted
them with tea in fine china. They knocked on
the doors in the humbler part of the village
and stood shivering by empty hearths. When

every maiden in the town had been seen, the search moved to the countryside. In small inns, women lined up to try their luck or hailed the group as they passed open fields.

Days passed and the search dragged on. But whether the ladies were from the town or the country, their excited reaction was always the same, and so was the outcome. The glass slipper never fit. On some, it was too small. On others, too large. It was too narrow, or too wide. No matter what the complaint, there was no doubt that they had yet to find the mystery princess.

"Enough folly," the Grand Duke said as he and the Captain rode. It had been weeks and still nothing. The two men were travel weary, their horses' coats covered in mud, their own clothes dirty and worn. Behind them, the guards followed, equally tired and hopeless. "Not a foot will suit this accursed shoe," the Grand Duke went on. "Time to head back to the palace, Captain."

The Captain sighed and turned his horse to go, but catching sight of a house down the road, he paused. "We're not done yet, Your Grace," he said, pointing.

Barely glancing in the direction of the Captain's finger, the Grand Duke waved at the house dismissively. "We have been there already," he said, agitated.

"We have not, Your Grace," the Captain said. The Captain was no fool. He had seen the way the Duke barely went through the motions, scoffing at the poorer girls and getting out of houses as quickly as possible. But this was Kit's future. There was no way the Captain was going to let him down.

The Grand Duke sneered at the Captain but reluctantly nodded. "Very well," he said. "We can tell His Highness that we have searched *every* house in the kingdom." Kicking his horse into a canter, they approached the house.

Unbeknown to either man, the house was in fact not just a house. It was Ella's house. And hearing the sound of hoofbeats, Anastasia and Drisella went wild with anticipation.

"Mother!" Anastasia cried from the parlour. "It's our chance!"

"Let them in!" Drisella shouted.

Unlike her daughters, Lady Tremaine was calm. She knew what would happen. Neither girl was the mystery princess. *She* was locked up in the attic. Yet her daughters acted as though they actually stood a chance. Not for the first time, she had to wonder how they had become such fools.

Sighing, Lady Tremaine walked to the door and opened it. She was surprised to see the Grand Duke at the head of the search party. There was a brief look of surprise on his face, as well. But then he composed himself and bowed deeply. She curtsied in return. Both pretended they'd never met before.

"A moment of your time, good lady," the Grand Duke said.

"Of course, Your Grace," Lady Tremaine calmly replied.

The Grand Duke took out a well-worn scroll and read, for the thousandth time, the proclamation and the command of the king: to try the glass slipper on every maiden in the kingdom until they found the foot it fit.

Nodding, Lady Tremaine called to Anastasia and Drisella.

"These are your daughters?" the Grand Duke asked, glancing at the two girls who fidgeted at their mother's side. Lady Tremaine nodded. "And they are the only maidens in the house?"

"Yes," Lady Tremaine said, pushing Drisella forward.

Taking the glass slipper off the cushion upon which it had been resting, the Captain of the Guard kneeled in front of Drisella. She lifted the hem of her skirt and began to squeeze her foot into the slipper – until her foot got stuck. The shoe was far too narrow. "How strange," Drisella said through clenched teeth as she continued to shove her foot inside the slipper. "It fitted so well at the ball." Then, with a yelp, she lost her balance and fell over.

"Enough!" the Grand Duke cried. He motioned to Anastasia.

Just as her sister had done, Anastasia lifted her foot. The Captain slid the slipper on. But where Drisella's foot had been too wide,

Anastasia's foot was just wide enough. For a brief moment, it looked like it might be a fit. And then everyone saw it: Anastasia's heel stuck out over the back of the slipper. Her foot was far too big.

The Grand Duke clapped his heels together. "Very well," he said. "Since there is no other maiden, our task is done." Then, for it was what he was *supposed* to say, he added, "The king will be disappointed."

"Ah, well, it is the way of the world," Lady Tremaine said, shrugging. She and the Grand Duke shared a barely perceptible nod. "But fate may yet be kind to us."

"Indeed, madam," the Duke replied. "You are as wise as you are beautiful."

With another bow, the Duke and the Captain turned and began to walk to their waiting horses. But as they did so, the Captain heard something. Pausing, he cocked his head and listened. There it was again: the very faint sound of someone singing – a *girl* singing. Whipping back round, he levelled his gaze at

Lady Tremaine. "Madam," he said, his tone warning. "Are you sure there is no other maiden in your house?"

Up in the attic, Ella was unaware that the Grand Duke and the Captain of the Guard were in the house. She didn't know that the other glass slipper was being tried on her stepsisters' feet or that Lady Tremaine and the Grand Duke had a plan in action. Her stepmother might have shattered her chances of ever seeing Kit again when she destroyed the slipper, but Ella wouldn't let her shatter her happiness.

She sat on her bed and sighed. She wouldn't allow herself to cry. Instead, she would focus on the good, just as her mother had taught her to do. She would hold on to her memories of Kit and remember the happier times from her childhood. She would think of her mother and father and the love they had given her, and that would keep her warm when winter came. Those thoughts would nourish her when she was hungry. While things had not gone her way, she knew she had kept her promises, and that was enough. It was freeing to let go of the pain and sorrow.

She began to move through the attic, her fingers brushing against the remnants of the toy butterfly, which was now gently laid on her bed. She leaned down and waved hello to Jacqueline and Gus, who twitched their whiskers happily. As she walked, she began to sing her mother's lullaby. "Lavender's green, dilly dilly," she sang, her voice soft and sweet. She approached the door and leaned against it, her voice growing stronger. "Lavender's blue.... You must love me, for I love you."

Chapter Fifteen

*I*n front of the house, the Captain stared at Lady Tremaine. The woman shifted uncomfortably as the singing continued.

"She's lying, Your Grace," the Captain said when Lady Tremaine continued to insist there was no one else inside.

"Nonsense," the Grand Duke snapped. He was tired of this pointless search and tired of the Captain. He grabbed the slipper and shoved it into the hands of a waiting guard. They had done what the king commanded – for the most part. How would Kit ever know they hadn't seen *every* maiden?

"Thank you," the guard said, accepting the slipper, his face hidden in the shadows of the cloak he wore.

The Grand Duke turned to go. But then the guard pulled back his cloak. The Duke gasped. Standing there, a witness to the whole scene, was Kit. "Your Highness," the Grand Duke cried. The other servants immediately bowed, as did the Captain and the other guards. Lady Tremaine's mouth dropped open as she sank into a curtsy.

(*I always did like that Kit. Such a clever boy!*)

Ignoring them all, Kit looked up at the house. "What sweet singing," he said. "It makes me want to tarry just a little. Captain, will you be so good as to investigate?"

The Grand Duke looked back and forth between the king and the Captain. He had been played! Kit had been there all along, watching him and making sure his orders were carried out. And the Captain had helped him! "Your Highness. I did not know," he said, trying to collect himself.

Kit looked at his friend. "Captain?"

The Captain knew exactly what Kit wanted. Taking Lady Tremaine by the arm, he pulled her towards the house. "Come along, then, madam," he said.

"It is a dirty servant, Your Highness," the woman called over her shoulder, dragging her feet. "A cinder girl!"

"He doesn't care about her station, does he?" the Captain said as they disappeared into the house. "He cares about her foot."

Ella was still singing when she heard the sound of the key turning in the lock. Her voice trailed off as the door swung open to reveal her stepmother and a man dressed in uniform.

"There," Lady Tremaine snarled. "No one of importance."

Ella recognized the man and his kind gaze. He had been in the forest and at the ball. If she remembered correctly, he was the Captain of the Guard – and a friend of Kit's! Her heart beat faster.

"We'll see about that," the Captain said to Lady Tremaine. Then he smiled at Ella. "Miss, you are requested and required to present yourself to the king."

Ella saw her stepmother's face turn red with rage. "I forbid you to do this!" Lady Tremaine screamed.

"And I forbid you to forbid her," the Captain countered. "Who are you to stop an officer of the king? Are you an empress? A saint? A deity?"

"I am her mother," Lady Tremaine declared.

Until that moment, Ella had been quiet, not daring to speak, not sure what was happening. But at the word *mother*, she stepped forward. She would not take Lady Tremaine ruining her mother's name. "You have never been, and you never will be, my mother," Ella said, her voice steely.

Nodding, the Captain held out his hand to Ella. "Come now, miss," he said.

Ella squared her shoulders and walked across the room, not even looking at her stepmother as she passed. But she couldn't avoid the woman's foul words, whispered in her ear: "Remember who you are, you wretch!"

Ella didn't respond. She kept walking right out of the attic and down the stairs, Lady Tremaine's last words echoing in her head. She was about to see Kit, which was both exciting and terrifying. For what if, when he saw her for who she really was, he didn't want her? What if her stepmother was right and she truly was no one? She stopped in the front hallway, her whole body shaking nervously, the Captain in front of her, her stepmother behind her.

She stared at the door for a moment. On the other side was her future. Good or bad, happily ever after or not. And in that moment, Ella knew that she would not let Lady Tremaine's words weaken her. She wasn't a nobody. She was someone who was kind, even to people as horrible as Lady Tremaine. She was someone who made sure the mice were fed, even if she herself was not. She was someone who was brave, someone who wasn't afraid to stand up for what was right. She was someone her mother and father would be proud of.

Taking a deep breath, Ella walked the last few steps and opened the front door. Standing on the other side was Kit. Her eyes met his.

"Who are you?" he asked, looking at her closely, an expression of recognition slowly spreading over his face.

"I am Cinderella," Ella said proudly. For Cinderella was a part of her now, and always would be. And she would no longer let it be a source of embarrassment. Instead, she would embrace it completely. Both as Ella and Cinderella, she'd become the person she wanted to be. "Your Highness, I am no princess. I have no carriage; I have no gowns; no parents and no dowry. I do not even know if that beautiful slipper will fit. But if it does, will you take me as I am – an honest girl who loves you?"

There was a silence. For a moment, Ella worried she had said too much. But then she saw delight in Kit's eyes. "I will," he said. Then, kneeling, he held out the glass slipper.

Slowly, Kit slid the shoe onto Ella's foot. The action felt familiar to both Kit and Ella as they thought back to the swing on that fateful night. There was a gasp from the onlookers as it slipped right on, a perfect fit. Raising his eyes to meet Ella's, Kit smiled. And in Kit's eyes, she saw what he saw. Not the glamorous girl from the ball, but the woman whom Kit, the king, loved. In his eyes, she was beautiful and radiant. She was strong and kind. She would be queen.

Rising to his feet, Kit took Ella's hand in his and squeezed. All around them, the servants and guards bowed. After a tense moment, even Lady Tremaine and her daughters curtsied, though they seemed pained to do so.

"Cinderella," Drisella began.

"Ella," Anastasia corrected, trying to get in her stepsister's good graces. "We are so very sorry!"

"Forgive us," Drisella cried.

Ella looked at the two girls and smiled. It was a smile that didn't make promises and left her stepsisters nervous. But Ella had already forgiven them. She could never treat them the way they had treated her. Still, for now, she would let them worry, just a little. After all, she wasn't perfect....

Epilogue

Ella and Kit stood quietly, hand in hand. In front of them were the two newest additions to the palace's royal portrait gallery – one of Ella's mother and one of her father. Ella smiled and squeezed Kit's hand. So much had changed in such a short time. Seeing her family there among Kit's, Ella felt love and happiness surge through her.

Kit smiled. "We must have a portrait of *you* painted," he teased, bringing them both back to the night of the ball, when they had stood in that very spot.

"Oh, no," Ella teased, playing along. "I do hate myself in paintings."

Kit put a hand to his heart, as though struck. "Be kind," he said, grinning.

"And have courage," Ella replied, this back and forth now a part of their daily routine. A way to remind themselves of all they had and all they could have lost if not for their strength and conviction.

"And all will be well," Kit finished.

They looked at the doors at the end of the gallery. "Are you ready?" Ella asked as they began to walk towards them.

"For anything," Kit replied. "So long as it's with you."

Together, they pushed the doors open and walked out into the sunshine, where their subjects awaited the royal wedding. And as they said their vows and promised to love and cherish each other, it was clear to all those who had gathered that this fairy tale would end as all fairy tales should ... with a happily ever after.

My Dearest Reader,

Can you see now why I've always loved this story above all others? It is the story I am most proud to have been a part of. It is a simple story, really. For at its core, it is a story about hearts closed off to love and hearts opened by love. It is a story of beauty, of pumpkins and horses and glass slippers. But most importantly, it is a story of kindness and the power of courage. And while I won't often admit there are powers out there greater than magic, I want you to remember this: a kind heart is the most powerful wand of all.

Now I must be off. A fairy godmother's work is never done.